GUARDING GUS

BOOK 1 OF THE GUS CHRONICLES

BY KARRYN NAGEL

PROMISE PRESS

Guarding Gus, by Karryn Nagel

This is a work of fiction. Names, characters, places, and incidents either are the product of the author's imagination or are used fictitiously. Any resemblance to actual persons, living or dead, events, or locales is entirely coincidental.

Cover design by Indicreates
Editing by Crab Editing
Book Formatting by Painted Wings Publishing Services
Typography by Amphi Studio

ISBN 978-0-9893-4517-0 (paperback)
ISBN 978-0-9893-4518-7 (ebook)
www.promisepress.org

DEDICATION

This book is dedicated to my cousin, Denise, my sister, Sierra, my other sister, Lisa, and my best friend Deepika. If anyone knows the profound value of a good man, it's these four.

This book is also dedicated to all the good guys out there who are practicing positive masculinity, looking after our veterans, and embracing our trans men.

Content Warnings

(** items are referenced, but not explored in detail)

- Aftermath of a gun-shoot out (no deaths)
- Transgender ftm topics such as passing etiquette, Latino family dynamics
- Criminal underground, threats of injury and gun violence (one minor injury)
- Vampires
- **References to veteran PTSD/military
- **Death of a grandparent
- **Gambling environment (casino)

Treasure Hunt Map

Our characters visit a total of 7 locations in the book, Guarding Gus. Each of these locations correspond to a real place in Portland, Oregon. Follow the below link to visit each one. The treasure lies in the delight of finding out where you might go next!

Disclaimer: Not every location is a mirror image of what's in the book, but there are surprises and delights in store. I hope you enjoy the adventure!

https://www.promisepress.org/treasurehuntguardinggus/

CHAPTER 1

Thursday 6 pm

Nico was standing in the gardening section of the cozily cluttered hardware store, considering a pair of stainless steel Satsuki shears for his personal bonsai plants. He had just picked up a pair by the teardrop handles that looked respectably sharp when he heard the unmistakable sound of gunshots outside. When Nico had entered the hardware store in the late September afternoon, the sun slanting across the parking lot, he made a point to note the entrances and exits — which was something he always did when he entered a new building. Dropping the shears on a nearby shelf, his heart pounding with anxiety, he raced down the aisle. Nico had a stocky build, but he stepped as deftly as a dancer around the trash cans of rakes, maneuvering past the towering, rotating display of seeds and the buckets of multi-colored pool noodles. He mentally thanked his security training as he bolted toward the front door. Heavy footfalls could be heard immediately behind him, and he instinctively turned, making eye contact with a muscular stranger whose friendly face had crinkled into the same concern.

Nico opened the door quickly and quietly, scanning the street. The stranger was close behind him but fanned out slightly to his right, hovering at his shoulder. It was clear that the conflict had just ended as the street was quiet, but only by a few seconds. There was a sour and angry smell in the air of discharged weapons, fear, and frustration. Nico and the stranger took cover about eight feet away from the hardware store entrance behind a city trash can.

The stranger, crouching down beside Nico, turned to him with a huge grin on his face, his green eyes vivid from the adrenaline. "You know what I said to myself this morning?" he said, somehow managing to sound soft but quite friendly. His voice had a tenor tone with a slight rasp. He continued on, "I said to myself, 'Self, what this afternoon really needs is a good old-fashioned shoot-out in the middle of the street.' What is this, the Wild, Wild West? Ridiculous."

"Someone could be hurt." Nico whispered urgently.

"Exactly my point," said the stranger, amused. "What on earth is out here that's worth risking human life for? A hardware store, a typewriter repair shop, and a couple of Hondas parked in the street? This doesn't make any sense."

As Nico scanned the street up and down, he reluctantly nodded his agreement that the scene in question was truly puzzling. His heart was still pounding a mile a minute, and the adrenaline made every detail sharper. He noticed a dirty sedan across the street that was parked at the curb, and there were two men running away from it towards a nearby alley. The stranger behind him leaned into his shoulder and said decisively, "I'm going after those guys to try to get to the bottom of this."

Nico only nodded, noticing that the huge arms and broad shoulders of the man revealed undiluted strength. He had the upper body build of an amateur weightlifter, a slender waist, with legs that matched his arms. He was a white guy in his late 30s and was growing a few days' worth of beard stubble. His hair was a sandy brown, cut short and neatly brushed. If he felt capable of handling those two men, then who was Nico to argue? The stranger took off like a shot on powerhouse legs at a surprisingly springy pace.

Nico was left alone and panned his vision to the left again. He noticed a navy blue SUV parked just a few cars down on his side of the street and saw that the tires had been shot out. The SUV was otherwise unmarked, which was strange. Was the intent of the attack to injure someone or to take them alive? As Nico swiveled back and forth looking for other threats in the road, he cautiously emerged from behind the trash can. He had determined that it was safe to approach the SUV, so he pulled out his cell phone to dial 911 in case anyone inside was injured.

Nico walked slowly towards the car, listening intently for any signs of distress from someone inside. His eyes continued to scan the street a few more times as he approached the back-left passenger door. The stranger was nowhere to be seen, so Nico braced himself for whatever he might find.

He opened the driver's door, but there was no one inside. Nico's heart was hammering, his vision had narrowed. Since he could see no one in the front passenger seat, he decided to move to behind the driver's door.

He opened the door gently and stood still in perfect disbelief. Sitting in a car seat, securely belted in, was a baby gargoyle. It was fast asleep.

CHAPTER 2

Thursday 6:15 pm

As Nico was standing in disbelief at the open passenger door, the muscled stranger rejoined him, slightly out of breath, to see what Nico had found. The stranger looked inside the SUV, looked back at Nico, and looked back inside the SUV.

"Oookkaaay. You don't see that every day," he said wryly.

Nico looked at the stranger and said, "Oh, good. You see it, too?"

"Oh, sure. That's a baby gargoyle," the stranger said confidently. He wore the same bemused expression from earlier.

"Have you seen many baby gargoyles in your life?" Nico asked calmly, though his insides were screaming at him, *THAT'S A MYTHICAL CREATURE.*

"Well, no, but I do believe they exist, so why not here, and why not...now, I guess?" the stranger said with a reasonable nodding of his head at his logical conclusion, absurd as it was.

"Right. Right." Nico said, pretending to stroke his chin thoughtfully. "And what do you suppose a baby gargoyle is doing in this car seat? Since you seem to have some insight on the matter." He deadpanned, gesturing with his hand, pointing to the situation as if they were discussing a tricky oil change.

The stranger ran a hand through his hair, "Well, the gargoyle thing is new to me, I'll admit. But ever since the vamps, werewolves, and fae came out last year — is that the right term, 'came out'?" He shrugged noncommittally. He didn't seem nearly as fazed as Nico. "I've met a few. Some of them are terrifying. Some are annoying. It's definitely been an adjustment."

Mr. Nonchalant seemed to realized that Nico was barely holding off panic. "Hey, it's cool. Is this your first interaction with magic? Because if it is, it's normal to feel a bit freaked. Although I have to say, I'm surprised you haven't encountered one until now. Didn't you see the new 'fairy air travel' signs above all the bike path lanes?" The stranger smiled at the ingeniousness of Multnomah's City Council to incorporate the flow of new species to the existing infrastructure. It wasn't perfect by any means, but it was a start.

Nico let out a short bark of laughter. "Yeah, I don't get out much. I am a bit of a homebody. I have noticed the changes to the city, but I just didn't think I'd meet any of them." Nico's nerves were starting to calm down, but his senses were still on high alert. "And, sorry, yes, is the answer to your question. It is my first encounter." he said slowly, staring at the gargoyle now. It was about two feet long, with a chubby belly and arms and legs of a light gray with dark green mottled spots down his slightly ridged back. Two enormously large and pointed ears were curled down while it slept.

"Well, I am not an expert on gargoyles, much less infant ones, but I would say that the handlers were probably transporting him as an exotic animal, and those dumbasses who got away from me were trying to steal him," the stranger said, pointing to the alleyway.

"Uh-huh. Can I just bring us back to the BABY GAR —" Nico was interrupted by the stranger brushing past him to reach out to the creature, gently cooing at his sleeping form.

"You poor thing! Did the bad men try to take you? We are going to protect you, so don't you worry about a thing." The broad shoulders blocked Nico's view entirely, but he could hear the stranger murmuring other comforting, nonsensical words, gently petting the baby's arm while it slept.

"We are going to what now?" said Nico, confused.

The stranger looked at him as if he was about to explain that square shapes go in square holes.

"First of all, you clearly have training in security, as demonstrated by your quick response and how you took cover immediately outside. That means that you care, and we both have a similar background. And that your first concern was for innocents." He had held up his hand and was ticking off points one by one. "Second," second finger, ticked, "you have now seen your first gargoyle, same with me, so we are in this together. Like, mythical creature buddies. Third," third finger got a flourishy tick, "we have to take care of this baby until we find who it belongs to, and lastly," he waved his hand around as the pinky finger came out, " those bad guys might come back, and we can't have THAT." He finished with finality.

Nico did work in security — of a fashion — but his self-preservation instincts kicked in, and he decided not to elaborate further unless necessary, so he ignored the first point but, instead, he chose to focus on the third point.

"Okay. That all makes sense. I do want to make sure the little...dude...is safe and gets home. I guess we should start by going through the SUV?" Nico proposed.

"Now you're talking!" the stranger clapped his hands together once, as if they had suddenly formed a pact.

"My name is Brant. It's nice to meet you." Brant reached out his hand to shake Nico's.

Nico hesitated, then shook the hand offered to him. Brant had a strong and confident handshake that matched his personality. Nico's grip was relaxed at first, but he took Brant's lead and they both stood there, pumping their respective handshake at the other until finally Brant broke away. He gave Nico a puzzled smile but said nothing.

Nico noticed his relaxed stance. He looked like a poster model for a Midwest farm hand. *Probably from Iowa*, Nico guessed.

As the two men explored the vehicle for clues, they were careful not to wake the baby who was snoring peacefully in the back seat. While Nico was searching the glove box, Brant spoke up from the trunk area.

"Do you know anything about this part of town?"

"No," said Nico. "I heard about this place at...work, and decided to check it out. I live across the river."

"Well, this is a territory of Viscidius Rubra, who is a nasty piece of work. He runs one half of the corrupt underbelly of this town. Bribery, gambling, extortion. Really seedy stuff. The other half is run by a person called 'The Volcano'." He frowned in disgust.

Nico was in way out of his depth. Crime lord? In Multnomah? His brain was screaming for him to get back to his plants, but instead he asked, "So what you're saying is that we interrupted a territory dispute?" Nico said, switching quietly to search the backseats and under the mats. He was so far afield from his comfort zone, he might as well be aboard a space shuttle. "Nothing here." he whispered, closing the side door as softly as he could. He walked around to stand near the gargoyle, his protective instincts telling him to stay as close as possible.

"I'm saying that besides the territory issue, which is worrying enough, I can't find any clues about this car or who owns the kid. There's a cage back here, but nothing else. Why did they move him to a car seat?" Brant mused aloud, puzzled. "Well, this is either Rubra's car, or The Volcano's. Although, now that I think of it, I think Rubra likes to collect exotic animals. So maybe this little crumpet was the next item for his zoo." He shook his head in disbelief. "I've had a run in or two with his security goons on occasion at work. I've even seen the man himself. In either case, we don't want to be here in case those thieves come back, and we need to get the little one somewhere safe." Brant's face turned thoughtful.

"Why don't we go back to my place and do some research so we can figure out our next step? I have some favors I could pull, maybe run the license plate with a detective buddy of mine," Brant said, clearly thrilled at the idea of an adventure. He had walked over to stand next to Nico. The door was open, and they both stared at the baby's face, ears, and claws. He had the chubby legs and arms of a newborn human, and his belly just begged to be tickled.

"Next step? I have work in a few days." Nico said in protest. His brain and heart were clearly at odds.

"Oh. Sure. Okay." Brant sounded hurt. "If you don't want to be gargoyle-rescue buddies, that's cool. I just thought you wanted to help."

Nico glanced to where the little one shifted fitfully in his sleep. He considered how risky it was going to be. Nico's new life had just begun to start, and this would be a threat to that. His brain warned him loudly not to get involved. But his heart just melted when he saw the infant. He knew what it was like to be judged for what he looked like. Uncharacteristically for Nico, who was not the type to make quick decisions, his heart had made the decision for him.

"Let's do it." He announced to Brant.

"Cool." Brant said, relief transparent in his voice. "Well, before we get started, we should stop for supplies."

"Supplies?" Nico asked. "What kind of supplies are we going to need to track down a powerful and well-connected criminal boss?"

"You'll see," said Brant.

Chapter 3

Thursday 6:30 pm

They spent the next several minutes trying to decide which car they were going to transfer the gargoyle to. Brant clearly knew the city better than Nico, but he had a 1970s vintage Ford truck that sat three on a good day. Nico had a more comfortable urban SUV, with four doors, a cozy trunk space, and access to set up the car seat. They left the transport crate from the back of the flat-tired SUV as it seemed too cruel to use after seeing the kid so comfortable and docile up front. The mystery of *why* there was a car seat in the first place was going to have to wait.

Nico felt strongly that he should be the one to wake the creature, given how restless and excitable Brant could be. He'd known the man a short while, and had already gathered that he was an extrovert. He liked Brant, but there was no denying that his energy was bouncy. Nico's more cautious nature would be better to gently wake the sleeping child.

Since neither of them had any experience with supernatural creatures, they decided to practice caution. Brant had argued that "He was just a lil guy, just a sweet little biscuit" and there was no way that babe was going to hurt anyone, but Nico reminded him firmly, "Safety first," especially since they'd established that neither one of them had heard of gargoyles, unless they count the stone statues at the tops of churches. Brant rolled his eyes behind Nico's back in response.

So there stood Brant behind Nico, ready to pull him back in case the creature woke up startled and became violent with those claws. Brant observed Nico's 5'9" stocky Latino frame, his soft black hair cut just over his ears. Brant noticed that he was a young guy, barely in his 30s, and had rounded shoulders. He had clearly started working out, if his toned arms were any indicator, but still had some softness to his frame. He was wearing a baggy T-shirt over jeans covered in dirt, anchored firmly with a pair of work boots. If someone were to pass by, it would look like two people preparing to jump off a cliff, standing at the edge together, braced feet, nerves jangling, psyching themselves up as they approached the precipice below.

Brant liked Nico as well and decided to play along with his absurd caution. He'd only known the guy for 15 minutes, but Nico clearly needed to relax, and if this helped him get there, so be it. Brant planted his feet and hovered his hands near Nico's waist. Nico reached out and gently shook the shoulder of the gargoyle.

The kid slept on, not a care in the world.

He reached out again and shook the shoulder again, this time a little more firmly. The infant's tail was curled next to him in the seat, and it reached up to swat his hand, slightly restless, but still unconscious.

He reached out a third time and shook the shoulder a little more firmly, this time humming a little lullaby under his breath, purely on instinct.

The gargoyle's eyes slowly and sleepily blinked a few times. One eye was a bright and lustrous gold. The other eye was a pearlescent silver, shining as boldly as a full moon at midnight. There was a ring of deep purple around the black irises. As soon as man and creature locked eyes, Nico felt a deep connection, a sense of loyalty and exhilaration. The gargoyle immediately reached his clawed hands out for Nico, and contrary to his normal instincts, Nico raised his arms to receive it.

Brant tugged on Nico. "What are you doing? I thought you said, 'Those claws could tear one of your sculpted arms clean off!'"

"There's no way it's going to hurt me. It wants to come with us." Nico said with a new confidence, gazing at the mismatched eyes with pure wonder.

"Are you sure?" said Brant, hesitant for once. He glanced at the gargoyle again, his gaze melting. Those eyes meant that this babe was likely to get anything it wanted. "Yeah, I get it. You're right."

Nico turned back to the gargoyle. "Come on, you adorable little apple blossom," he said, affecting the coaxing tones of a new father.

"What did you say?" asked Brant.

"Oh, nothing." Nico replied hastily, unbuckling the safety belt and lifting the gargoyle in the air. It revealed three ragged teeth in a goofy grin. It's tongue lolled out of his mouth and it blinked again slowly. It's skin was leathery like a lizard's, but soft as new pine needles. It stretched a tiny set of wings that unfurled from behind the shoulder blades. As Nico lifted it into the air, he saw a tail unfurl from underneath it. The entire creature was *enchanting*.

Brant freed the car seat and they transferred the two over to Nico's car. Brant grabbed a bright yellow, plushie bumblebee from the crate in the trunk before he had collapsed it and handed the toy to the kid, who gurgled happily and grasped his thumb in return.

Brant climbed into the back passenger seat and Nico got in the driver seat. Nico turned and said, "Okay, what is this special stop that you want to make for supplies?"

Brant grinned wickedly but only gave Nico turn-by-turn directions through the evening dusk, refusing to answer completely. The gargoyle was alert now and watched the scenery going by with great interest, looking up at the tops of the modest apartment buildings, scanning the neon-signed bowling alley and other boutiques as they whizzed by. The peaks of the mountain range were still visible against the soft pink clouds of dusk.

After just a few minutes on city streets, Nico pulled up next to a pastel, brightly colored store, with a flashing neon sign that blinked OPEN. He turned to Brant in utter amazement.

"You can't be serious. This is what you meant by supplies?" he asked, incredulous.

"What? My sister and I came here a lot when she was pregnant. My niece loved everything we got from here. Trust me, we need this place." Brant answered cheerfully, bounding out of the car and rushing to get to the creature before Nico had even removed his seat belt.

"Unbelievable." Nico muttered, staring up at the painted logo over the massive front doors. The sign read Babies R Us.

CHAPTER 4

They paused briefly as the automatic doors swooshed open, Nico trailing slightly behind. Brant made his way confidently to the center of the store carrying the youngling in his arms. The customer service desk was located in a crescent moon pattern facing the front of the store, both the heart and the dumping ground of the retail experience for both employee and customer. Brant knew better and politely greeted a young Asian person who looked to be in their 20s with short blue hair, dressed in a long-sleeved black T shirt, black jeans, with a tacky store-logo'd vest worn over the top. The name tag read "Xavi," and they were wearing a bright green button declaring "Pronouns are THEY/THEM." They looked curiously at the gargoyle.

"Hello! Is that a teacup dragon plushie? Where did you get it?" Xavi leaned in to touch what they thought was a doll and saw the baby's head swivel to meet their eyes.

"Oh wow, is that thing alive?!" Xavi shrieked and took a step back. Several reactions crossed their face at once — astonishment, excitement, then back to some semblance of composure. "I'm sorry. I've never seen a magical gargoyle before. So sorry." They took another breath, their eyes never leaving Brant's arms. "Let me try this again. How can I help you today?" Xavi asked, the words tumbled out as they looked curiously, craning over the counter.

"Yes to the help. We just found this little orphan and are on our way to try to find the owner," Brant spoke, a mix of bravado and hesitation evident in his voice. Nico felt relieved that he was not the only one who was feeling freaked out. Brant continued, "Normally we would hit up the pet store, but they are closed, and I thought we should try here. Since we don't know anything about it's care, let's start with clothes and any parenting books you'd recommend. We do have a car seat and a plushy toy, though."

"How old is…it?" they asked.

"Based on how tall it is, I'd say less than 6 months." Brant hazarded a guess. Nico tugged on his arm.

"How tall it is?! That's no way to measure age!" he whispered, exasperated.

"Maybe not, but we have to start somewhere, and this rep already has more knowledge in their pinky than we have put together, so unless you want to take the lead on this, then we need the help." Brant whispered back, reasonably.

Xavi spoke up, gesturing to the gargoyle. "Actually, height is a reasonable indicator for human babies. This one, I'm not sure. But it's a start, as he said." they gestured vaguely at Brant, who was looking smug.

Nico turned to the sales person. "Isn't there a famous baby book by a Dr. Somebody or other? Couldn't we start with that?" he asked.

"Yes! You are thinking of 'What to Suspect when you are Suspecting'," they gestured to a nearby shelf, drawing them over to it.

"Great. We will take that." Nico replied. "We are also going to need footwear. Let's base it off of what fits, not a *guess*." Nico glared at Brant.

"Are you always this logical?" Brant grumbled but was immediately distracted by the miniature dresses. He handed the toddler to Nico unceremoniously and wandered off, presumably to look for a gift for his niece.

Nico turned back to the sales person. "I like your hair," he said, attempting to make conversation. It was so hard as an introvert to conceal his awkwardness, but Nico had been making a concerted effort lately to practice small talk.

"Oh, thanks!" Xavi said, leading him towards the clothing section. "So, what is the little…dude's name?" they asked.

Nico and the sales associate simultaneously studied the gargoyle. The babe stared back at them both, wide-eyed and happy, taking in all the surroundings. Then it opened its mouth and croaked out a high-pitched, "Gustopher!"

Nico and Xavi gasped in shock and both began speaking at once.

"DID YOU HEAR THAT—"

"OMG, WHAT A CUTE NAME, I CANNOT EVE—"

"BRANT, GET OVER HERE!" Nico shouted.

Brant came running and arrived in seconds, almost barreling into the three of them.

"I heard something! Did the little one speak? What did it say? Was it Dada?!" Brant was out of breath with excitement.

Nico took a calming breath. "It said, 'Gustopher.' I think that's its name." Nico's eyes were lit up, all trace of caution gone.

Brant gave a huge grin and leaned down to baby Gustopher. "What an awesome name! Can I call you Gus? I'm so sorry I missed it!" this last comment he directed at Nico, never taking his eyes off Gus. Brant was so downcast that Nico reached out and patted him on the shoulder awkwardly.

"Thanks, man. I appreciate that." Brant acknowledged the gesture, patting Nico's hand on his arm.

Meanwhile, the sales associate gesticulated in the air as if fanning their face from a bayou heat wave.

"I'm going to be okay. No, really. I will. Whew. Okay. That was an epic level of adorableness! Let's get you both the rest of what you need before I pass out," Xavi snickered at Nico and Brant. "So, boy, girl, other, bonus?" The associate was studying Gus's features.

Nico was not enthused to begin a discussion of the complexities of gender in the middle of a baby store where lurking, judgey parents would overhear and feel compelled to soapbox their views for the world, and was even less open to the idea of sharing with Brant that he himself was mid-transition.

Even lifting the tail and checking down below felt indignant, and what did it matter anyway? The question of gender wasn't the most pressing need. They decided to go with neutral colors for the clothes, at least for now. Nico was insistent that Gustopher have some clothes with flowers and trees on it, while Brant picked out clothes with patterns of food and desserts.

Selecting the clothes was easy enough; they held up the outfits to the little body to see what would fit, picking out sleeveless dresses, shirts, pants, booties, hats, scarves, and onesies just for good measure. There was an awkward discussion as they realized they would have to cut holes for the wings, but Nico volunteered to do this, as he was more adept with a pair of scissors than Brant. The question of food was a trickier one, as human formula wasn't likely to work, but they didn't want to risk having nothing on hand, so they picked it up anyway. A few helpful parents chimed in and assisted with the general instructions on how to mix powdered formula with slightly warm water and with what ratios.

Xavi asked them with the directness of having dealt with thousands of new parents and without the slightest tone of judgement, "Does either of you have any experience with babies?"

Brant shrugged his shoulders in a noncommittal 'kind of' way and Nico shook his head.

"I'll take that as a No," they said dryly. Both men had firmly denied the need for diapers, but one particular grandma with dyed red hair and dimples insisted they get some "just in case." She was bossy and endearing, and both men were relieved to have the assistance.

She taught Nico and Brant how to attach the diapers, and how to get a baby to take a bottle (there were many wild assumptions at this point of what Gus ate, and what to do with what came...after). Bewildered fathers had been a staple of baby stores since the first one ever opened.

Xavi was back at the customer service desk when Nico and Brant finally walked up, piling their things on the countertop. As they were ringing items up in the cash register, they asked, "So how long have you two wanted to have kids?" Xavi continued scanning, then packing up the last of their items into bags. Brant had headed towards the exit with Gus on his hip as Nico was finishing the sale.

"No, no, noooooo. We are not together," Nico replied quickly. "We actually just met...today."

"Oh! I'm sorry I presumed. It just seems like you two know each other well. My apologies." they said, embarrassed.

"Please, don't be sorry. It's understandable. Even though we just met, he seems like a pretty decent guy. Besides, he's so…sunny." Nico said it like it was a failing, but was smiling. Xavi laughed.

"Yeah, sunny people are the *worst*," they said conspiratorially. Nico joined in, chuckling.

Brant called from the sliding front doors, where he was already bouncing out through them with Gustopher.

"Oh! One more thing. You are going to need this," they dashed to a donation box that was near the front door, pulling out a contraption for wearing a baby on your chest. It had straps and a soft-shelled center section for allowing the baby's arms and legs to swing free, but still support their back, head, and bottom. "These were gifted, and you will want to keep the little one close." They replied, beaming. Nico tested it by placing the straps over his shoulders gingerly, walking over to Brant, taking Gus, and carefully placing the gargoyle in the front. His heart contracted pleasantly. Gustopher waved their hind legs, bouncing and enjoying the sensation.

"Thank you so much. As you can tell, I'm out of my depth." Nico said, ruefully.

"You are already off to a great start on fostering," they said, smiling.

"Let's GO!" Brant pleaded from the doorway.

"Good luck." they said.

"Thanks."

As Nico approached the car, he extracted Gus and handed the baby off to Brant, who buckled all the safety straps and situated himself in the front passenger seat.

"Baby Gustopher!" Brant sighed wistfully. "What an unusual name. Are you ready to go, little dude?" Brant directed this to the gargoyle, turning in his seat. He gasped, then smirked and turned back to the front, barely restraining his silent laughter.

"What is it? Nico said. "What's wrong?"

"See for yourself." Brant said, barely able to get the words out. "Exactly like my niece. Kids, man."

Nico unbuckled and turned awkwardly around.

Gustopher had ripped off all of the clothes: hat, scarf, T-shirt, pants, onesie. All the fabric was shredded from its sharp claws and strewn across the back seat and floor.

Nico noticed the booties were still on — clean, fuzzy, and bright yellow. Baby Gus grinned at the two men, tongue hanging playfully from its mouth while squeezing the plushie bee with a tight grip, waving it about in contentment.

Nico sighed as Brant howled with laughter.

Chapter 5

Thursday 7:30-8:30 pm

Nico liked the idea of going to Brant's house to re-group. Brant had the advantage of a 3-story house with an enclosed basement, whereas Nico lived in an apartment complex with curious neighbors. They could keep a closer eye on Gus, try to do some research, and Brant had a spare room for Nico to crash in if he needed it.

They doubled back to retrieve Brant's car from the hardware store's neighborhood before caravanning to his house. Brant lived in an area of town known for resting on the top of a dormant caldera, which was much scarier than it sounded. As they carpooled, Nico checked on Gus in the rearview mirror obsessively, but the baby seemed to enjoy the drive, occasional chuff noises coming from the back seat. Nico tried several times to get Gustopher to speak again, but the gargoyle just looked at him with those shining eyes, grinning and waving his claws around in lazy circles.

They finally turned down a residential street, quiet and pleasant. Brant's house was the fifth one down on the left, and he gestured out the window for Nico to pull into the driveway. A side door to the house was clearly evident. Nico pulled in, and Brant walked up to meet him, his car parked on the street.

Brant unlocked the side door, while Nico extracted baby Gus from the back seat, and placed it gently into the baby carrier.

As Nico walked in, he was struck with the most incredible smell of baked goods he had ever experienced in his life. It carried notes of lemon, cinnamon, vanilla, and maple sugar. There were enormous containers of flour, sugar, baking soda, and baking powder, all securely fastened with metal clasps and labeled with Sharpie pen in a neat hand. There was a massive rectangular island with storage underneath, crowded with baking bowls of all sizes and materials; he had wood, metal, plastic, and ceramic. Gus immediately squirmed in the carrier, and as soon as Nico put the gargoyle down, Gus fell to pulling out the plastic mixing bowls on the floor and playing with them. Brant swiftly lifted the ceramic bowls up and away, tucking them somewhere safe. The rest of the kitchen was bright and friendly, and the only item that seemed unusual was the double ovens. The youngling and Nico were both taking deep breaths and savoring the waves of pure contentment. When Nico did open his eyes, Brant was beaming.

"This is my happy place. I have a bit of an obsession," he said sheepishly.

"Are you joking? I can't remember the last time I smelled something so delicious. What an incredible place. Did you put those ovens in yourself?" Nico asked, amazed.

Brant laughed. "No, I'm not quite that gifted. The contractor put those in. I am working on expanding my skills, but it's mostly carpentry right now. I did do a lot of other things here, though." He walked around the island, pointing out the small improvements to the kitchen that would make a foodie blush. Quiet closing doors. Magnetic racks for utensils, a hanging pot rack. Hidden compartments for food waste and recycling. Retractable shelving everywhere. But the piece de resistance was a ceiling-to-floor, multiple-layered, rotating organizer spice cabinet that Brant revered the way other people fell to hushed tones in the Long Room Library at Trinity College.

While the kitchen was clearly the pride and joy of the house, the rest of the home was decently kept. The master bedroom was on the first floor, with its own bathroom. The living room had an enormous TV mounted above a fireplace, a recliner, a big squashy couch, and loveseat. It had a friendly and sunny vibe, just like Brant himself. The intoxicating smell permeated everywhere.

Upstairs was a midsized spare bedroom with a skylight, a small office, and another full bathroom. Nico spied some military paraphernalia on the wall of the office, but Brant quickly shut the door and mumbled something about it not being clean enough for guests. Nico took the hint and didn't bring it up.

As they explored the basement, there was a workout area with a mat, weights, and speaker system. A washer and dryer were tucked against the wall with a table for folding clothes in front of it, mirroring the setup in the kitchen upstairs. A tall stack of deep storage plastic bins, neatly labeled, were next to the laundry area. Nico could make out some camping equipment on the floor in front of the bins, still covered in dry mud from its last excursion.

Gus bounced along on Nico's chest this whole time, growing more alert as they explored each room. He grew fidgety, despite Nico's attempts to pacify the baby with rocking, reassurances, or playing with the soft pads under the claws.

"Let's go upstairs to the living room and see what we can find online," Brant said, noting Gus's impatience. "I'm sure we can put him down to run around for a bit."

"He?" Nico asked. "What makes you think Gus is a 'he'?"

"I don't know, and I don't actually think it matters, but for now, it's easier to just pick one. I choose 'he' because that's what we are. Once we know for sure, or unless Gus tells us, will that work?"

Nico was secretly relieved that there was now a strong chance that Brant would be okay with him being trans but was still feeling cautious. He did agree regarding Gus, though. It would be rude to keep calling Gus "it". This babe had won his way into their hearts already. Nico had rescued a stray dog once, and while the feeling was similar, this was much stronger. He wondered if it had to do with Gus being magical, or a gargoyle, or both.

"Yeah, that works great," Nico replied as he walked up the basement stairs, heading for the living room. As he was getting settled and freeing Gus, who was jiggling like a Jell-O mold in an earthquake at this point, Brant appeared with his laptop computer from his office on the second floor. Gustopher leapt onto the ground on all fours, kicking a leg out behind him and galloping around the room, dashing off to the kitchen.

"Be careful in there!" Brant called. "Don't you dare break anything, kid!"

Brant opened his laptop and started researching the little bit of information they had: the license plate of the SUV. With no way to assist, Nico asked for a pen and paper and started making notes of all the information they had learned so far. After a few minutes, he started perusing the baby book they had bought and could hear Gus scurrying from room to room, and other than some suspicious toilet splashing, the toddler remained remarkably easy to care for. They worked in silence for a good 30 minutes, both of them engrossed with their own activities.

Finally, Brant gave a sigh. "I'm hitting some dead-ends. I am going to have to call my buddy at the police station. This'll just take a minute." He gestured to his bedroom, indicating he'd be back momentarily, and Nico gestured to the laptop. Brant nodded his approval, then stepped into his bedroom to make his calls.

Nico spent a fruitless 10 minutes online looking for information about live gargoyles and found nothing. They were going to have to fly blind when it came to his care, which did not put Nico's mind at ease. He didn't want to risk Gus's health just because they both didn't know what to do. Where did Gus come from? Where was his family? How did Rubra get a hold of him? Nico was so distracted by the enormity of what to do next, he had just started to turn back to his notes when he realized it was eerily quiet in the house. *Wasn't this a bad sign with babies?* he thought uneasily. His fear grew as he searched the main floor of the house — no Gus. He dashed up the stairs and came up empty-handed from the spare room and bathroom. He noticed a sliver of light coming from the office and approached cautiously. Brant had firmly closed this door, Nico was sure of it.

He opened the door slowly, scanning the room. Gus was sitting quietly on the floor, gazing up at a display on the wall. Nico walked closer and saw that Gus wasn't hurt and the room appeared undisturbed, but still, the babe gazed up at the display again and then looked meaningfully at Nico. Nico studied the display closer. It had a picture of Brant in full Army regalia, standing stiff as a board, looking stern and intimidating and totally unlike the man Nico had met today. There was a medal in the display along with his bar of rank, but Nico didn't know what this signified. He just knew that Brant didn't want them both to see it. He scooped up Gus gently and started to head out of the office, but when he turned back, Brant was standing in the doorway.

Brant liked Nico, he liked Gus particularly, and he liked the idea of a new adventure to take his mind off the food truck construction and his usual broody thoughts. The part he didn't like was having to talk to one of his unit again at the police station. He had given his blood, sweat, tears, and darn near his soul to the United States government when he fought in the Iraqi War for three tours over five years, and he was done with that life. Becoming a civilian again was somehow harder than being a soldier, but ever since he had discovered his love — and knack — for baking, he'd never looked back. He had clung to it the way a rock climber does to a shear wall face, only two fingers and the desperate, time-frozen will to live keeping you alive.

Baking was always a good investment. People enjoyed baked goods when they were celebrating small wins or recovering from big losses; like the post office, rain or shine — although in this mountain town, it was more rain than shine — there was no slow season. It was creative, experimental, and a wide range of options were available from every culture on

Earth. And more importantly, it kept Brant from going off the deep end.

Brant had entered the service quite young and impressionable, straight out of his sheltered Midwestern small town. It's the age-old tale; boy has dreams of glory, boy tries to impress his family, boy gets his optimism dashed on the battlefield. There was nothing special about what happened to Brant. He had seen enough senselessness to know that he only survived because of a mix of faint common sense and random dumb luck. Not everyone in his unit was so lucky.

The thing that made Brant special was *how* he was coping with it.

When he left home, he had a shitty apartment, no life experience or partner to speak of and no direction. When he came home, his grandmother had died and left him this beautiful house, her recipe book, and a chance to escape the pit in his heart that the war had left there.

Brant had struggled for the last 10 months, every day scraping by, perfecting his recipes, throwing himself into caring for the house, and working towards a modest goal: open a food truck, specifically, a cookie truck. He wanted to offer cookies, *his cookies,* out of a mobile truck. That was it. Seemed simple, huh? But living alone was so much harder than people made it seem, especially for an extrovert like Brant.

He struggled with getting away from his reoccurring dreams of the war at night, and he struggled towards his bakery truck dreams during the day. He had been considering getting a foster dog in the last few weeks just to cope but wasn't sure if he was ready. Then he met Nico and Gus. The whole existence of Gustopher, from the moment Brant had seen the little guy, had brought a sense of childlike wonder that was unmatched in its innocence and delight. Brant would protect Gus, and this feeling, at all costs.

As Brant stood in the doorway of his office (which he was certain he had locked), his face fell as he saw Gus and Nico in his private space. Nico had his back facing to Brant. Brant had met a few Latino guys with him on tour, but they hadn't been close.

Brant didn't want to share this part of his life with strangers. He wanted to pretend that *that* life didn't happen. But Gustopher was staring at Brant, his little arms reaching out to be held. His gaze was compassionate, full of wisdom beyond his years. He seemed to sense Brant's anguish and was radiating a sense of envelopment. Brant felt *held* all over, which was an accomplishment, as he was a big guy. Suddenly, the idea of keeping secrets from these two seemed ridiculous. He couldn't do it. He *shouldn't* do it. After all, that's what new life was about. Making a new start.

"I got a lead," was all Brant could manage to say. "Let's go downstairs and I'll brief you." He turned away from Nico and Gus, wincing at the choice of words. They were so cold; the military lingo was slipping in. He would have to watch that.

Nico looked stricken but followed him down the stairs quietly.

They all got settled in the living room, and before anyone else could, Brant took a deep breath and began first.

"I'm not mad. Seriously. I don't know what it is about this little dude, but, *man*, he's got a hold of me. He's cracking me open like an egg." He gave a snort. "Baker pun. Not a bad one.

Will have to remember that." He shook his head like he was clearing his ears of water.

Brant continued. "Listen. I was in the military. It was brutal; it nearly destroyed me. I have had some dark days, let me tell you, and calling my buddy at the station, who is firmly in denial and pointedly NOT dealing with it, brought some things up. But," he paused, collecting his thoughts, "I have a new life now that I have fought hard to get, and I'll be damned if something is going to threaten that." He said this with finality. He had kept his eyes on the floor the whole time, but he looked up, hoping, at best, to see acceptance and, at worst, to see discomfort.

Nico was smiling broadly, and Gus's tongue was lolling out of his mouth. Both of them were looking at Brant with a mixture of admiration, friendship, and pride.

"I have something to talk to you about, too," Nico said simply.

As Brant listened intently to Nico share about his transition, his mind was crowded with questions about the process of what it must be like to realize that you are not really a girl, but a boy — a man, he corrected himself silently. He wasn't sure what was okay to ask, and he didn't want to offend his new friend. He considered where his questions were coming from and found that they were mostly about wanting details that felt *very* private to ask a relative stranger. He filed most of his questions under "none of his business" and landed on the most important one of all, the one that had to be answered.

"How can I support you?" he asked Nico, who had finished speaking and was now looking at Gus, listening actively from Nico's lap.

Nico felt his heart constrict at the clear nonjudgement in that one sentence. He considered the response when he told his family; his abuelita had stood up from the table and walked off to her room. His mother and father had both shifted uncomfortably, and his father finally spoke and said, "Sure, whatever, son," placing a disapproving emphasis on the last word. Just weeks prior, his father had been saying that this was a phase that would pass, while his mother looked on sorrowfully.

But at least his mother's face in that moment had taken on some acceptance. She was clearly conflicted by the response from her mother and her husband, but a determined glint had come into her eye, and she had winked at Nico before rising from the table. Nico could hear her say down the hall, "Come with me, mi amor, and we are going to have a talk about your new son." His mother had also placed an emphasis on the last word, but this had some protective bite to it. It gave Nico's heart a tiny flame of happiness in the echo of darkness.

Listening to Brant's question had given Nico the same flame, this time a little stronger. He didn't know this man, he didn't know his troubles. Hell, he was barely figuring out his new and truest self, and this new friend had a better sense of "live and let live" than his own father. He slumped in his seat, feeling relief cascade over him in waterfall waves. He felt he had crossed a canyon by simply lifting his feet and was soaring across.

"I appreciate that, man. I really do. I tell you what. Why don't we watch each others' backs?" Nico said, smiling and scratching Gus's head at the same time.

"Deal," said Brant, smiling back.

Nico spoke again, but this time with more eagerness than before at the idea of their mission. "So, what did your buddy have to share?"

Brant's face turned somber, but he said, "The license plates registered as belonging to Viscidius Rubra and that is both good for us and bad for us. Good for us because that tells us that Gustopher does belong to him and his stupid menagerie, and we should try to find him as soon as possible. Even if that's not what we want to do," he finished. Gustopher had crawled into Brant's lap at this point. Brant looked down, directing his next question to the gargoyle's big ears flapping about.

"I don't suppose you have anything to say about that?"

Gus's eyes were closed, but he peeked open one lid and glanced up at Brant. Gus was either not understanding Brant or choosing not to answer. Brant shrugged.

Nico brought Brant's attention back by puzzling aloud, "So what's the 'bad for us' part? And wait, why do we have to return Gus if we know this guy is a bad dude?" Nico was struggling to understand.

Brant sighed unhappily. "Well, the truth is, I don't know how he treats his animals. For all I know, they live good lives. So I guess it really comes down to if you want to deal with the consequences of making Rubra angry by trying to keep Gus. And he will be angry, believe me. I for one don't believe in stealing other people's stuff. I would have to clearly see that Gus is in the wrong hands. I don't see any signs of neglect or abuse on him. I mean, I think this little guy is incredible, but..." He petted Gus between the ears affectionately as he trailed off. "What do you think?"

Nico considered for a moment. The lines of ownership for animals in the human world were clear. There were domesticated pets and exotic animals. Exotics could be, and sometimes were, kept as pets by the wealthy, which is what he thought was the situation here. But a rare creature, especially one that was clearly new, even in the magical world? Nico felt at a loss of where to even begin and who to ask much less the legalities. His head was swimming.

Nico nodded at Brant. "I agree with you, for now. Until Gustopher tells us something, or we see that it's a bad idea, let's proceed with the Found Dog policy. Let's return Gus to Rubra and not risk his wrath. If something shows us along the way that he would end up abused, we'll...cross that bridge when we get there."

Brant rubbed absentmindedly at the top of his nose and sighed again. "There's a second problem, logistically. He has several dozen businesses around town, and he likes to visit them all. So finding him will be a little bit tricky. We can probably rule out the day venues; he enjoys his nighttime money-makers." Brant frowned, concentrating on the notes he'd taken during the call.

"He also likes to name his businesses after hockey teams. He's a massive hockey fan." Nico remembered something in his pocket, retrieved it, and opened his hand to reveal a matchbook from a bar called "MinnWild". He had found it in the SUV but didn't think it was important. He held it out to Brant, who examined it. It was expensive. The matchstick heads were dark green, and they could still smell the earthy wood that made the base of the matchstick itself.

Nico put two and two together. "Let me guess, Minnesota?" he said.

"Now you got it. Once you see it, you'll see it everywhere." Brant rolled his eyes.

"I guess it's as good a place as any to start."

They packed up Gus into Nico's car, a more palpable trust between all three of them — two men, and a baby gargoyle in tow.

CHAPTER 6

Thursday 8:30 pm

MinnWild was located in Multnomah's Old Town, across the river from the east side. The city boasted over 12 bridges that crossed the Whilamut River, and they drove over the Fernside Bridge, which held two attractions —it was a road that spanned the whole central part of the city straight out to the suburbs, and it had an iconic neon sign of a leaping deer in bright white, beaming like a lighthouse across treacherous shores. The sun had long since dipped low over the western hills that housed the famed rose garden, but even against the deepening blue sky, Nico was struck by the lush tree line as always. It distracted his mind from the returning apprehension, and he silently cataloged the trees by species to fight off his intrusive thoughts.

"Hello? You all right, dude?" Brant said, giving Nico a shove in the arm.

"Huh? Yeah, sorry, drifted off. I was distracted by the trees." Nico said, offhandedly.

"The trees? What for?" Brant asked, confused.

Nico's emotions were surprising even himself. Why had he opened up about his transition, but was having trouble admitting that he loved green, growing things? He avoided the subject by changing topics. He could analyze his bizarre trust issues in private. "So, where exactly is this place?" Nico said hurriedly.

Brant noted the topic change and rolled with it. He knew that trust was a two-way street, and if Nico had things to hide, there was no need to give away the farm all at once. It was going to be a long night anyway. So as Nico navigated the one-way streets in Chinatown, Brant gave directions to the bar, and Nico parked a few spots from the entrance. As the car's engine grew quiet, Brant looked at Nico from the side, asking, "So you don't know this place? It's extremely popular."

Nico replied warily, "I don't get out much once I'm done with work. I'm more of a stay-at-home type."

"Oh. Where do you work?" Brant asked conversationally. Look, he tried. He waited a whole five minutes. But patience never was one of his virtues.

Nico shifted uncomfortably. "It's…not far from here. Near downtown. I work in hotel security. Pretty boring, actually." Nico didn't like lying to Brant, but he just wasn't ready for the ridicule of his job, which most men looked down on. Brant noticed that Nico clearly didn't like talking about himself.

Nico changed the subject again, steering back towards Brant. "What about you? Where do you work?" he asked, glancing away from a spot in the road he'd been gazing at.

Now it was Brant's turn to look evasive. "I am just a bouncer. My job is to break up fights and keep out minors." He replied, shrugging. "Still. I have dreams of my own, and will be able to quit my job in the next few months."

"What dream is that—" Nico started to ask but was interrupted.

"This is it. Let's go. " Brant said as he exited the car. Unbeknownst to Nico, Brant also was on the receiving end of teasing about his own job and was relieved to avoid the next question.

Nico spotted the sign that read MinnWild as he locked the car, glowing green against the black night sky. The sun had set completely by this point, and the typical buzz of nightlife activity had already begun. The line to wait for table service was growing to 30 people, the universal promise of a good meal tempting patrons inside.

Brant turned to Nico. "Should we bring Gus or should we leave him here? Do you think he's okay on his own?" He glanced back at the gargoyle, who had been lulled to sleep on the drive over. It was like magic, one moment he was awake and running around the house, and the next, he was snoring as the night was long, clutching a toy bee.

"I think it's safest if we leave him here. We don't know what those guys will do, and they will likely take the route of apical dominance."

Brant gave Nico a blank look. "Apical what now?"

"We don't want to overplay our hand," Nico said quickly.

Nico and Brant approached the patina'd copper on the metal door with intricate floral scrollwork and pulled hard on the double, curved wood handles, where a host was taking down names and looking as though their night was already off to a bad start. Nico smiled tentatively. The host did not return it.

"Did you want to add your names to the list? It's a two-hour wait." the host said, in a clear effort to discourage them from staying,

"No thanks. We are looking for the owner."

The host bristled and stood a little straighter. "The owner is not on site this evening," he said smoothly, looking them both up and down and deciding that what he saw was a disappointment. "Frankly, he likely wouldn't see either of you, anyway."

Brant shifted aggressively next to Nico, flexing his arms. "It's so loud out here," he said sweetly. "I must have *misheard* you insult my friend and me here—," Nico grabbed Brant's arm.

"We are trying to return something of the owner's that he...misplaced," Nico said, putting the emphasis on the last word. His mother would be proud of the irony.

"How nice for you," the host drolled sarcastically. "I suggest you take your lost baggage and find a thrift shop to sell it at. I think the flea market opens on Saturday at 9." he spat, turning away from them to help a large party to a table.

Brant was still fuming over the host's rudeness when he was suddenly distracted by someone at the bar. From their vantage point in the foyer, Nico could make out an atmosphere unlike anything he'd seen before. Large, structural, gleaming mahogany wood pieces stretched like muscle tissue across the ceiling, roping down in long, curvaceous sinews. The effect was like a grooved yet liquid underground cave system and it was both otherworldly and cozy at the same time. Warm yellow lighting backlit rows upon rows of colorful bottles and liquids. Nico briefly felt like he was in a potions shop. The music was a soft milonga as a nod to the style of Spanish Art Nouveau, and the vibe was contentment and quality. Despite not being a drinker, even Nico was impressed. It was an architectural marvel, a cultural hub, and boasted a wide library of spirits.

"Hold up. This might be helpful," Brant said, gesturing with his chin. Nico followed his line of sight to where an older man sat on a tall stool, his posture that of a recently-fed predator. He was in his mid-50s, with salt and pepper hair and with an olive skin tone, and wore an open expression. His eyes, even from this distance, were shrewd. He had a jawline that could cut glass — it was so sharp and pronounced. He raised his eyebrows and smiled in invitation, and his teeth were so white that there was a shine on them. Nico couldn't be sure, but he thought he saw the man's teeth had little points on them.

Nico turned to Brant.

"Before you say a word," Brant interrupted, "just remember that we are at a dead end, in a lion's den. We need a lead. This guy might know something. He looks like the kind of guy who would know Rubra." He finished.

Nico sighed. "Okay, well, I am going to go check on Gustopher, so I'll be right back."

Brant nodded. "Good idea. Wouldn't want the little guy to wake up and not see his two dads there." He grinned at the thought.

Nico left through the front, the host glaring at him.

Brant approached the stranger at the bar, but as he got closer, the hairs on the back of his neck started to stand up. His instincts were telling him not to approach, but he felt certain this guy knew something. He had that cat-who-swallowed-a-canary look. Struggling to keep his voice friendly, he said, "Hey, how's it going?" as he arrived at the bar. Brant looked downright shoddy in his casual and baggy clothes next to the polish of the other man.

The bartender came over, but Brant shook his head. She was appraising the well-dressed man and as she caught his eye, she smiled lazily at him. He returned the smile and winked at her.

Turning back to Brant, the stranger cocked his head and studied Brant, grinning mischievously from the corner of his mouth.

"So, I hear you are looking for the owner?" the man said smoothly. He spoke with a pronounced French accent.

"How did you hear—"

"I have excellent hearing," the stranger said, smiling wider at some private joke, his pointed teeth clearly visible up close. Definitely a vampire. He continued, "I am in town on vacation and would love a little adventure; I crave a new experience! I believe you have something of value in your car for him?" the stranger questioned, all mock innocence.

Brant could feel the danger emanating from him. A ripple of icy shivers went down his back that he struggled to conceal. His fragile trust was shattered when the vampire emphasized "of value", and Brant decided to take his chances elsewhere. Gus was not to be trusted around this man. For all he knew, the vampire was lying and was working for The Volcano. This could be a second attempt to abduct the kid. He'd explain to Nico that the stranger had nothing of value to share. His face had turned serious and was full of clear mistrust when Nico walked up and rejoined them.

"Gus is still sleeping. He's dead to the world." Nico said, clearly relieved. He turned to the stranger. "Not sure if introductions have gone around, but I'm Nico." Nico put out his hand the same way Brant had, straight out in front of him, fully extended.

The stranger gave a full, wide smile, still radiating a private amusement, but grasped Nico's hand and shook it down firmly, just once.

"I am Remi. As I was just telling your friend, I am interested in helping you find the owner of — Gus, is that the name?" he said, his face blank with mild curiosity, but a wicked gleam had entered his eyes.

All of Brant's military training was screaming alarm bells inside, and he burst out, "I haven't told you a DAMN thing, and yet you seem to know all about us. Now why is that?" Brant demanded in a low voice, shifting his stance and broadening his shoulders.

Nico adjusted from the friendly to the now-threatening situation in rapid succession.

He took a long look at the vampire, weighing if they could trust him or not. He didn't know why, but he did. He trusted him. "Whatever your intentions are," Nico said carefully, "the two of us are not welcome here, so we were just leaving. Right, Brant?" Nico risked a glance away from Remi to Brant's face. His friend was clearly angry but was nodding his agreement at the thought of leaving.

Just as Nico and Brant were about to step away, three burly-looking security guards approached, looking conspicuously out of place in head-to-toe black. Clearly Rubra's men. Their presence rolled in like a thunderstorm, and the presence of authority put a serious damper on the bar's lively atmosphere.

"Time to go, Vampire." One of the goons said, gesturing to the street. "You've had your fun among the humans. Not sure why the boss allowed you in, in the first place." He gave a disapproving grunt of disgust.

Remi stood and took a step toward the guard. The man took an instinctive step back, and Remi's smile was dangerous.

"Of course. Please convey my gratitude to your boss for the...hospitality," he said flippantly.

One of the guards muttered to the other, and they snickered in clear ridicule.

Remi suddenly relaxed his posture, slumping his shoulders and bowing down his head.

The guards, Nico, and Brant all stared at Remi's abrupt change in demeanor. He went as limp as a wet handkerchief.

He then suddenly jumped up in a little hop, waving his hands in the air, and gyrating his hips back and forth like Elvis. He hopped, scooted, and even gestured to the female bartender, who winked and shook her head in amazement.

Remi's dancing was ridiculous and goofy, and a subtle tension that was present in the patrons near him visibly relaxed. His face was ecstatic, and the guards shoved each other with laughter, leaning in to exchange jokes about his absurd display.

Ever so subtly, Remi waved one of his hands, low, in a gesture of dismissal that Brant caught. Brant made eye contact with the vampire, and the message was clear: Remi was causing a distraction so Nico and Brant could leave without further harassment.

As they were slowly backing away and more and more security guards and patrons came out to watch Remi's spectacle performance, Remi cocked his head to the side a few times, smiled in his dangerous way, and concluded with a bow to the jeers, cheers and clapping of the entire bar.

Nico and Brant were regrouping outside when Remi approached them.

"So. Now that I've sufficiently distracted the guards, I can share what I overheard—" he started. Brant raised a hand in protest, but Nico stopped him.

"Brant, I know you don't trust him, but at this point, we need the information. And frankly, I've never met a vampire, much less one with such impressive dance moves." Nico smiled genuinely at Remi, who gave a silly smile in return. Nico had *really* enjoyed the display inside, and it was his firm opinion that anyone who is light on his feet is light in his heart. He couldn't even explain it, but he just trusted him. Perhaps it was all the exposure to the supernatural, but he was remarkably sanguine at this point. For an introvert.

Remi sighed dramatically, clearly for effect. "Everyone expects me to be such a brooding and bloodthirsty killer. I VANT to DWAIN your BLOOD and all that nonsense. I mean, I drink as needed, but," he shrugged noncommittally, "I'm not tortured. What I *truly* crave at my age is new experiences. I can help in many ways, c' va, and it seems like you could use an extra hand." He waved his hands in the air, jazz hands fluttering.

Brant's suspicion was not completely satisfied, but since Remi had helped them, he wasn't one to hold a grudge, so he repressed a grin and affected a more stern face. "Okay, fine. So did you use your super senses to hear some secret bad guy chatter?" he demanded with his arms crossed.

Nico shot him a look of exasperation that clearly said, COOL IT. Brant relaxed his tense stance and opened his arms in a gesture of reconciliation.

Remi grinned again. "I like you two. You are like Brie and Parmigiano."

Seeing their confused expressions he said, "Opposites. What do humans say? Pickles and carrots?"

"Peas and carrots," said Brant, chuckling despite himself.

"Yes, peas and carrots. One is mushy and tart, one is crunchy but sweet. At least, that's what I remember." Remi frowned in concentration.

"So while I was dancing — beautifully, I might add — I overheard the guards talking about how I would look at their boss's dance club, The Golden Knight. They also did not believe your story of a lost object, though they are very stupid, I assure you. I presume their boss might be at this club. I've met Rubra, and he is not a man that humans should trifle with. I can tell you, he will be very displeased to learn of their carelessness in not speaking with you further." Remi finished, beaming. "See? I am useful. May I see the treasure now?" He clapped his hands together in a pleading gesture, which looked suspiciously like he was making fun of them, except that his face showed completely genuine interest.

Brant and Nico both sighed simultaneously.

"Brace yourself," Nico said, opening the car door. "Have you ever seen a baby gargoy—" Nico's lips were suddenly pushed shut like a duck bill, held ever so gently closed by two fingers in a pinch from Remi, as the vampire drew an unnecessary breath of total surprise.

"Mon Dieu, I haven't seen a baby in hundreds of years. I cannot believe they still exist!" he whispered, covering his mouth with his free hand. He gazed in abject admiration and love, his eyes roaming to the yellow booties and shaking with silent laughter.

He removed his hand from Nico's face and stood taller, abruptly.

"Not to be dramatic, gentlemen, but what you have here is priceless beyond measure. I would gladly swear upon pain of daylight to help you in your noble quest to return him home safely — if, of course, that is the baby's wish — and will now swear my blood oath to you both." Remi began to lower himself to his knees in the street while Brant and Nico watched with gaped mouths.

"Is this strictly necessary?" Brant said, finally. He looked both shocked and amused.

Remi suddenly stood, all trace of antics gone, his face a fury. "There are men nearby, strangers; not the same guards from within. I suspect they want to take the youngling. They are nearly here. They stink of greed and fear. " He straightened his stance, his face going completely blank. "I will dispatch them." Nico barely had time to say, "Don't kill them!" before Remi was gone, evaporating from where he stood like a final curl of smoke from a snuffed candle.

While the-blur-that-was-their-new-friend Remi was racing around their car, dispatching of the threat, Nico had gotten in and started the engine. Brant climbed in the back seat with Gustopher, who had just started to wake. They heard a few thuds, a grunt, an audible "WHY WON'T YOU" and then the muffled sounds of surprise and retreating feet fading, and in another instant, Remi was back and inside the car, no noise preceding his opening of the front passenger door. Brant was so startled that he yelled, "Snickerdoodle!" from the back seat. Both Nico and Remi turned to stare at Brant in open astonishment.

"What was THAT?" Nico asked, directing the question both to Remi and Brant.

Remi shrugged his sculpted shoulders elegantly. "You told me not to kill them. I figured, for you, I will just scare them. Or knock them out. It's easy when you are as old as I am." He batted his eyes, innocently. Nico stared and let out an abrupt bark of disbelieving laughter. This night was so *weird*.

"And you. Did you shout a cookie?" Nico asked Brant, as both he and Remi turned in their seat to stare at the embarrassed grin on Brant's face.

"I wasn't completely honest earlier about what I do for a living," Brant said, looking down.

"Yeah, I could tell but I didn't want to push," Nico replied, also looking down.

"Hey, guys," Remi said.

Brant was saying, his voice plaintive, "I get a lot of flack for my work, so I wasn't straight with you earlier. I want to come clean about my real job, maybe compare tactics on personal protection skills if we are going to look after Gus, at least for now."

"There's something happening to the ba—" Remi started.

Nico had been feeling guilty ever since he had lied earlier. "Yeah, I lied to you before. I do have some training in security, but I'm not really in hotel secur—" Nico was saying to his bellybutton.

"THE BABY. IS TURNING. TO STONE." Remi said.

Chapter 7

Thursday 10 pm

There was going to be a point when, someday, Nico would look back at the absolute time warp/alternate reality of three fellas, one of whom was a vampire (despite knowing they existed, now he'd actually met one; cool, cool, no big deal), and a baby gargoyle (also existed, Nico's world was tempted to crumble, but hey, why fall apart now when things was just getting interesting), trying to find its owner *while being attacked*, and just laugh and laugh. You know, laugh in the easy manner in which people laugh when they truly aren't trying to impress or scare each other. When they're slapping their legs, kicking their feet in the air, snot coming out of their noses and falling on the ground, snorting and hiccupping, their cheeks aching, because it's just such a silly thing to *say*, much less to *be* in that situation.

Nico wasn't there yet because the scene was in complete chaos.

He had popped out of the car and grabbed Gustopher, cradling him over his shoulder, pacing in a four-foot tight oval, shaking him up and down as if the stone layer would just come loose and flake off of him like shale. Remi had disappeared entirely in a flash that was so jarring it was as though he'd never been there. Brant had also moved quickly, heading straight to the trunk, yelling incomprehensible instructions and concern from the back of the car where the hatch was already flipped up. He was throwing things, crashing, and came rushing around the corner and slammed into Nico just as he had completed another tight oval. Nico's mind had gone a complete blank, and a buzzing in his ears made his brain register the distant fact that he was in shock. Nico fumbled Gustopher, nearly dropping the now-20-pound statue, and both men let out high-pitched squeaks of panic.

Brant, desperate, said, "This will work!" while dousing Gus in a lumpy concoction of formula and water, straight over his head, wings, and once-floppy ears.

Nico and Brant watched, their hearts frozen.

Nothing happened. Gustopher was as still as his statuary kin, and now dripping with a gloopy, milky mess.

Nico went back to pacing, clutching the baby in his arms, wiping away the formula mud while his mind raced. He tried to think of what a gargoyle might need, his anxiety and panic threatening to overwhelm his nervous system. Brant had gone back to the trunk, muttering to himself, paging through the baby book furiously, occasionally saying in a strangled voice, "That should have worked!"

Remi appeared suddenly beside the car, startling both of them. Brant let out a surprised "Buckle!" and once again, Nico and Remi stared at him for his odd choice of exclamation. Nico gestured to Remi's hands. "What is that?"

Remi was holding a bird in one hand, and a bat in the other. He looked confused.

"Gus needs to eat. Gargoyles turn to stone when they are hungry. This is what he eats." he said calmly as if explaining the way the moon rises and sets. He held up the bewildered animals to Gustopher's nose and waved them back and forth experimentally. Brant and Nico looked on, both experiencing wild happiness at Remi's return and an awful splinter of despair if this didn't work. Slowly, as if he were a wax mold melting, Gustopher came back to life, nose first working furiously at sniffing both creatures. He turned away from the bat and immediately swallowed the bird in one gulp.

"We thought you had left us," Nico said weakly. He was clearly coming down from the anxiety tidal wave. He felt rubbery and leaned on the car for support. Brant nodded his agreement, not trusting himself to speak. Gustopher was looking back and forth expectantly between all three of the men for a second helping.

Remi bristled. "Of course, I wouldn't leave you. But I assumed you both didn't know what he eats, and I have been around enough over the years to know that because they live on the top of churches and cathedrals, they live off of birds, sometimes bats too, that are flying by. I thought it was obvious." Remi explained, looking almost disappointed.

"Yes, of course. Obvious," said Brant, a full dollop of sarcasm present. Brant's face had fallen, and Nico asked him, "What's wrong?"

Brant replied, "I feel like I was just handed the Manley Cup, and then it was stolen."

Nico considered pretending he knew what that was and changed his mind. "And the Manley Cup is...?" he prompted Brant hopefully.

A look of disbelief crossed Brant's face. "Are you serious? It's only one of the most iconic trophies in the whole world. It's for hockey." As Nico continued to shake his head in ignorance, Brant let out an exasperated sigh. "Don't worry, I'll catch you up," Brant assured him.

"I will go get him a few more. Bee, Are, Bee, is that what we say now?" Remi mused before disappearing again.

"BRB. It stands for 'be right back'," Nico said to the thin air. *Well, at least Gus is back to normal, and as a fun side project, I get to teach a vampire current cultural slang,* he thought darkly.

Remi returned shortly with a few more birds, which Gus immediately ate happily. As the men began to calm down and get back in the vehicle, Nico cleared his throat. "I think it's time that we all come clean with each other."

Brant and Remi nodded in unison.

Nico continued, "I have something I need to tell you both and if you want me to leave after I share this with you, I understand. I don't want to risk Gus's life, and it's only fair that I be honest." he said stiffly. Brant and Remi waited in silence.

"I'm not really in hotel security. I did do a security training course, and I guess it stuck with me, because of the hardware store," he trailed off, looking at Brant, who's face held only attentive encouragement. "But I do work in security...of a fashion. Just not with...humans." Brant looked confused, while Remi took a sudden interest. "No, nothing supernatural." He sighed. "I work at a Japanese botanical garden, and I guard the bonsai exhibit. People are always trying to touch the trees, some of which are over 100 years old. People can be very inconsiderate. I have volunteered there for years because of my extensive gardening background, but they offered me a job to keep people from accidentally breaking branches off, knocking them over, or just trying to steal them. Many of them are on loan from other countries, and they are seen as prized exhibits."

Nico searched Brant's face for confusion, hurt, or anger that Nico wasn't a "real" security guard. He had really grown to like Brant, and he didn't want to hide his life from him. Surprisingly, neither one of them seemed like they were about to make fun, or even angry that he'd lied. As a matter of fact, both looked relieved.

Brant was the first to speak. He sounded deeply irritated. "You mean people try to fuck with those little works of art with the tiny blossoms and the tiny branches and things? I'm not much of a flower guy, but I have seen them up close, and they are incredible. I learned all about them on a date once at the botanical garden. Must be the same place, huh? Dude, Bonsai is a revered Japanese art form!" Brant's voice had risen, and he turned his head away, angry. When he turned back, his voice rang with disapproval. "That's messed up." He said flatly, looking at Nico, his eyebrows raised. After a moment, he said, "I'm glad you are there to protect them. Some of them are so elaborate. That's so cool. I freaking love bonsai. They are amazing." Brant said, giving him a look of admiration.

Remi also spoke, his voice uncharacteristically low. "I am 382 years old. I have seen many wonders of the human world. Only two other things compare to the majesty of the bonsai," he said solemnly, utterly genuine in his seriousness. "You are doing very important work."

Nico felt the tension in his soul leave his body. He lost feeling in his hands. It had been so, so hard to tell Brant about his transition. He had only told a handful of people, and they were all people that he knew. Now, two confessions in one night? *It's got to be a full moon or something,* he thought. Most men he'd met worked very traditionally masculine jobs or sat behind a desk. Nico enjoyed watching Nature's cycles. He could understand them; birth, growth, death. He loved working at the gardens. He struggled to find other men who enjoyed just nurturing and coaxing life along. While talking about one's job may not be a big deal for others, it was another hurdle for Nico when it came to finding friends. He was still composing himself when Brant spoke.

"Yeah, um. Here's the thing. I lied as well. I'm not really a bouncer. Well, sort of? I guard this cookie shop downtown that's in a pretty unsavory neighborhood. There are all kinds of people who are either high or mentally unwell, and they try to smash up the windows, harass the patrons, or just cause a scene in front of the shop. But it's crazy popular, though. That's how I found out about all this territory bullcrap between Rubra and the Volcano. And...well, fell in love with baking. The girls there give me all kinds of recipes." He hesitated, then seemed to come to a decision. His voice took on a determined tone. "I'm working on remodeling a food truck right now so that I can drive around, park at the food truck lots, and sell cookies of my own. There's absolutely nothing like the smell of fresh cinnamon." He sighed wistfully.

Nico and Remi both beamed at Brant. After a long moment of studying Nico and Remi carefully, Brant returned their smiles with a bashful grin. A small burp came out of Gustopher, and the guys all chuckled at the release of tension. Remi piped up with a note of delight in his voice. "I guess it's the moment of true confessions for all. Yes, it's true, I'm here on vacation, but you should know that I work the night shift at the secret cheese caves in Wisconsin. Before I was turned into a vampire, I was a cheese monger and it is my passion."

He finished with a practiced ease, but there was something behind his eyes that Nico caught. Something...unfinished. Nico flashed Remi a look of sympathy.

"Is that one of the wonders of humanity?" Nico asked lightly, bringing things back to a lighter subject.

"Mais bien sur!" Remi replied, laughing. "So we are all guards, but of a more colorful kind, n'est-ce pas?" said Remi. "It's wonderful that Fate has brought us together. Or truly, is it Fate? Or is it Gus? Perhaps his magic brings out the secrets in us all." Nico considered this last sentiment, finally connecting that the divulging of confidences might be related to Gus himself.

Remi gazed fondly at the youngling, still burping his dinner. "Shall we continue on?" Remi asked, reaching over and stroking Gustopher's ears, the gargoyle making happy gravelly noises.

CHAPTER 8

Thursday 11:00 pm

Brant was enjoying the more trusting camaraderie in the car, but there were still several problems he could see that were present. That was the thing about being ex-military. Your mind was constantly surveying the landscape for threat assessment, having to make snap judgements about trustworthiness, always staying on high alert. While this part of being a civilian was a relief, to let go of that state of tension, it never really completely left. So he honed in on the useful and said, "Hey guys, before we decide our next move, there's a very real issue that we need a solution for and I am not exactly thrilled about it."

Nico's face fell into a wary expression. Brant reassured him, "The little tyke has had some dinner, right? So that means it's on its way through his system and..." He let his companions fill in the rest.

Remi spoke first, "You mean he needs to wash down his dinner with some lizards? Perhaps some rabbit?" he said playfully.

Brant studied his new companion. He didn't know the vampire well enough to see if he was kidding or not. His sense of humor clearly ran very hot and cold. Remi was nothing like he thought a vampire would be. Why on earth would a vampire care about cheese? Brant was confused by the man and wanted to solve the mystery. He still didn't trust Remi, but the quick thinking when Gus turned to stone and the absurdity of the evening had been a funhouse contraption ride so far, and Brant was enjoying himself. He hadn't felt this kind of kinship since his last tour.

"No." he deadpanned, rolling his eyes at Nico. Nico turned away to hide his smile. Brant regained his composure to say, "Remi, Gus is going to need to go to the little gargoyle's bathroom soon."

Remi exclaimed, "Ah! Yes, the distasteful act of evacuation!" as if he were a circus ringmaster introducing the next act. "I am happy to say, 'sounds like a you-problem, Boyo.'" He was so proud of his slang, Nico didn't have the heart to remind him that everyone was pitching in. Equally. He wasn't sure he wanted to argue with Remi over such a small point. Though, was it a small point?

Brant continued, "We can deal with *that* subject shortly, but the other issue we have is exposure. Those men that Remi dispatched —" he gave a begrudging nod to the vampire, who bowed his head in honored acknowledgement, "— were probably The Volcano's, and are trying to take Gus to make a statement to Rubra. We need to lay low while we look for him. I think we should re-group at my place. I can call my detective friend back and try to get some leads." He looked at Remi now. "Are you able to go out during the day?" Brant asked bluntly.

Now it was Remi's turn to look cagey. He shifted in his seat, seeming to wrestle with the idea of disclosing another confidence. "It is true, I cannot go out into the direct sun," he said with hesitation.

"Okay then, I suggest we turn in for the night and try again tomorrow evening. Unless Nico has any ideas?" Brant asked. He was hoping Nico had a brilliant solution, because even though he had come up with the idea to return to his house, he wasn't sure that he wanted Remi inside.

Nico looked at him with a rueful grin. "You said we were on a mission. This is it. We definitely need to make sure we can handle Gus while we track down Viscidius, and in the meantime, maybe I could help taste test some of those cookies?" Nico was struggling to look nonchalant, but the clear desire for sweet treats was evident in his smile.

Brant barked out a harumphing laugh. "Operation: Baby Rescue, now in motion. Destination: Classified." He laughed at what the other soldiers in his unit would say if they could hear him now.

12 am-overnight

There was a palpable lightness in the drive back to Brant's house. Nico felt as if a great wall that had always obstructed his daily view had been removed from his line of sight, and there were lush meadows as far as the eye could see. The peace radiated off of him like sunlight.

Brant was even more relaxed and jovial than normal, which was saying something considering how playful he was. He bubbled with excitement as he shared that outside of trying new baking recipes, his favorite hobby was crocheting. He was already describing outfits that he wanted to make for

Gustopher, clearly forgetting the shredded clothes that still lay on the car floor.

Remi had also become more relaxed and was sharing some of the details of his peculiar job at the caves. Since no one back home had wanted to take the night shifts in the long Wisconsin winters, it fell to him and just one other person to guard the caves at night. Remi spent an enormous amount of time reading books, listening to podcasts, learning all the ways of the outside world. Out of boredom a few years ago, he had discovered the resurgence of roller skating in some Midwestern cities and decided to test out his dexterity on the wide, smooth concrete floors of the warehouse. This odd fact didn't phase Nico or Brant in the slightest, but both of their eyebrows had shot up as they pictured it.

To Nico's mind, the subject of the security profession was something he'd given a lot of thought to, and he suspected Brant had as well. It was the reason why he hadn't gone into a more traditional security role, because like so many others dominated by men, it was one of the toxic spaces where hate and misogyny could thrive, but Nico had finally found his people. Those who protected the diverse elements of our world, items deemed valuable not because they held a particular political position, power, or military rank, but because they were prized for their beauty, for their innovation, or for the artistry and culture of what that object represented.

Nico pondered what other men would make of Gustopher, and it made him feel even more protective of the little one.

As the four of them pulled into Brant's driveway, Remi stood formally at the side entrance door. He was clearly waiting for an invitation. Nico had already bustled Gus and what was left of the shopping into the house, while Brant looked at Remi for a long, long moment without speaking. Both men seemed to be assessing each other. The silence continued and Nico glanced at the two from the kitchen island where he was unloading some bags. Gus was sitting on the floor on all fours, watching them. The moment stretched and Nico was beginning to think that Brant was going to refuse Remi's entry. Gus lumbered over the threshold, looking up and pulling gently on Remi's pant leg. Remi bent down, breaking eye contact with Brant. He spoke softly to the gargoyle. "It's all right, le bebe Terroir. He sees me as a threat."

Brant couldn't refuse Gus. He wanted to say no — there was definitely something the vampire was holding back — but it didn't matter. He would have to figure that out at a later time. "Please come in," he said, resigned. Gus gave a leap of joy, and ran into the house. Remi stepped across the doorway, relief just evident at the corners of his eyes.

As soon as Remi crossed the threshold, however, Brant held up a hand in the air over Remi's chest. "Listen. I don't know what you are hiding. Eventually it's going to come out. You don't have to tell me now, but," Brant watched Gus leaping around on his couch, "you will need to tell me soon. A vampire hanging out in Wisconsin? With your proclivities? I'm not an idiot. Either you are running from or running to something. Like I said, you don't have to tell me now, but you can't bring your mess into the kid's life."

Remi met his eyes, and for the first time, respect shone there. He nodded his head in acquiescence.

"I will divulge what is safe for you to know, but first thing tomorrow afternoon, oui?" He said lightly. Brant gave him a tight, reserved look, and walked away.

Now that they were in a safer place, both literally and figuratively, they could turn their attention to getting Gus settled in for what was left of the night. Nico's tired brain was skeptical of Gus's bathroom situation — which had yet to be sorted out — but at least they had baby wipes on hand. Remi had stepped back outside to bring in the rest of Gus's supplies, Brant had gone to the kitchen to deal with his feelings about having a vampire in the house, and Nico was trying to figure out the best place to set the young one. In the guest room with him? He was going to be collapsing soon from exhaustion, so probably not. Brant's room? That seemed too far away from where Nico would be on the second floor, and wherever Remi would be sleeping.

Nico stepped into the kitchen after his assessment. "Hey, I need to sleep soon; I am beat. Do you think Remi could sleep with Gus overnight in the basement? The three of you seem nocturnal, and I could do the day shift."

"That sounds good. I will have some fresh items for you when you wake up." Brant smiled faintly, but the worry was still evident in his face as he scooped out flour into a measuring cup.

"What is it?" Nico asked, yawning. "Sorry."

"I worry about what he's holding back," Brant said, pitching his voice low. "I just don't know if *what* he's holding back might get any of us hurt. My protection vibes are off the charts," Brant finished, his flour sifter bouncing against his flat hand held vertically.

Nico's eyebrows shot up. "Oh, you too? I thought it was just me. Must be the dormant parental gene," Nico said, stifling another yawn. "Or it could be that thing Remi said in the car, about Gus's magic affecting us? Well, I will talk to

Remi and get Gus set up. Thanks for letting me crash. I'm going to grab a spare shirt and toothbrush from my trunk and go to bed. Good night."

"Night," said Brant, already reaching for the spice wall. Just the thought of a freshly baked anything in the morning gave Nico a cared-for feeling. Brant was right; baking was magic. He was looking forward to tomorrow — or, later today, he corrected himself tiredly.

Nico directed Remi to move the items to the basement, and the vampire had a corner set up in moments. He turned to Nico. "I overheard the plan. I can stay down here with Gus. I do not require anything, and there are no windows down here." Remi hesitated. "Thank you." It seemed like he wanted to say more, but when he didn't, Nico responded, confused. "For what?"

Remi gazed at Gus but did not respond. Nico was too exhausted to beat around the bush and was not interested in brokering a peace between the two men. "Gus wanted you here. That's good enough for me. Just don't kill us," he was struggling to find the words, "or bring anything here that might kill us, and we're good."

Remi gazed at Nico, his stare growing unnerving. Finally, he whispered, "I assure you, young man, the danger is yet to come." Nico started to speak, but Remi refused to say anything further, turning away.

Nico gave up and started climbing the basement stairs, hardly able to stifle another yawn. "Okkkaaaay. Thanks for the cryptic hints? That won't haunt me at all tonight." he said sarcastically. "Good luck anyway, I'll be up around 6," he replied, his footsteps echoing on the wooden stairs. The baby squeaked from the floor of his portable playpen, where he sat on a pile of blankets with his plushie bee. Nico turned back on the stairs, pausing. "You're okay! I will see you in the morning! Tío Remi and Brant will take care of you!" Gus squeaked again in what sounded like an acknowledgment, but Nico was too tired to process. He waved goodnight to everyone and collapsed on the guest bed, fully clothed.

Brant had spent a strange middle of the night/morning with Remi and Gus. While he was working in the kitchen, Remi had gone out to get more food for the kid, which was actually very considerate given that it was 1:30 in the morning, and finding wild birds or an animal supply store open at this hour was a tall order. His instincts had settled into his gut as he waited to hear what the vampire was keeping from them; was Remi helping out to divert attention away from himself, or was he genuinely trying? Like Nico, Brant had decided to leave the decision to Gus. If the kid was safe, the rest could work itself out later. And really, what did it matter, if they only had the little dude for a few days? Not *that* much could happen, his mind reasoned, as his hands put the final orange frosting glaze on top of the fresh cinnamon rolls he had baked.

After Remi had retrieved more food for the little gargoyle, he had come upstairs and settled into the living room with the TV on, leaving the basement door open in case Gus wanted to go down to nap. The kid had no such interest but did continue to explore the house, occasionally playing with Remi or Brant by pulling on their pants or running his ridged back up against their legs. Brant finished the cinnamon rolls, putting most of them in the warmer for later, scooping one for himself onto a small plate, and decided to try to appease his suspicions by joining Remi.

The two men sat in front of the TV as the rerun of the 11 pm broadcast announced that a few local members of the hockey team, who had won the championship this year and would be celebrating with the coveted Manley Cup, might be seen around town with the historic trophy over the next few days. Brant listened with interest, as hockey was one of the sports he enjoyed watching. He felt a surge of regional pride that his team had won. He'd been hoping since he was a kid to see the Manley Cup up close one day.

As he was watching the TV and enjoying the tang of the orange with the soft, sweet cinnamon bread, Brant snuck a glance over and saw Remi was just as interested. "What is it, man?" he asked.

"Oh! Hockey is fascinating! We did not have such things in my human time. I love to glide on the ground in my rolling skates, it feels like floating." He looked sad for a moment. "I have tried to ice skate, but no one is ever around when I do this at night."

Brant felt a stab of sadness at the idea of someone who liked to try new things doing them on their own. It took more guts to do that, and he respected the idea, even if the visual made him want to laugh. He stifled that, as he could see it would be hurtful. Remi was just nothing, nothing like he thought a vampire would be.

"Are all of your kind like you? So comfortable with human hobbies?" he said, priding himself on finding a diplomatic way to put it.

Remi's expression turned dark, almost angry. Mostly, he looked frustrated and sad. "No," he said with regret. "Very few see things...like me." He gathered up Gustopher from off the floor where he was slowly shredding a cheap blanket with his claws (thankfully Brant hadn't put out his grandma's knitted blankets, and he made a mental note to get more soft things for the baby to safely destroy) and placed Gus on his lap while he gently extracted the fabric scraps. Gus and Remi were staring at one another with open affection, and Brant felt another stab of sadness at his paranoia. But something still persisted in the back of his mind. He trusted Gus, but he trusted his instincts as well. They had saved him many, many times.

Remi pulled his gaze away from Gus and looked thoughtfully at Brant.

"Have you ever baked parmesan and rosemary madeleines?"

The faint autumn sun was peaking through the thin curtains in the guest room as Nico awoke. He had slept surprisingly well for only getting six hours of sleep, and in a strange bed, no less. The mattress under his line of drool was firm but supportive, and the room boasted a simple bed, dresser, side table, and a few posters of the local hockey team mixed with some landscapes that were clearly hand-painted. He stretched and rolled over, wondering how the early morning hours had gone between the two prickly men. He glanced at his watch and saw it was nearly 6 am. He rubbed his face vigorously, shaking off the sleepies and pulling on his clean shirt until he could wash up. He needed to check on Gustopher first.

Nico walked out to the living room quietly, his socked feet testing the hardwood for creaks. He hit a few, but they were quiet ones, the kind you'd expect in an older house. He looked over to the couch and saw Brant passed out on his back, Gus asleep on his chest, both of them napping and looking like the most natural pairing on Earth. *If only Michelangelo was here to sculpt these two,* thought Nico. *We could call it Baker's Repose.* Remi was nowhere in sight, but Nico figured that with the sun coming up, the vampire would be tucked away downstairs.

Suddenly a smell hit Nico's nose and pulled him bodily towards the kitchen. He was mesmerized, captivated by the happy assault on his senses. He could still feel the heat coming from the closed oven door, and he spied two marvelously piled serving platters with what looked like glazed cinnamon rolls and a small, buttery-looking cookie with rosemary leaves in it. That explained the savory punch in the air. Nico couldn't resist; he reached out to try one of the delectable cookies and sank his teeth into a cheesy, buttery, savory soft bit of heaven. The rosemary had just the barest herbal top note, and the parmesan cheese flooded his mouth and made it water. He groaned involuntarily and let out a small, happy laugh into his cupped palm. He was still entrenched in the various flavors when he spotted the note from Brant.

'Remi and I came to terms, a little, this AM, and I hope the result of that is as good as the smell. Need your HONEST notes on that when I get up at 1, btw. I spoke to my [illegible] at the station, he gave us another place to try. Told him about the attack; he said be careful. We need Remi, for now.'

There were smeared fingerprints in the corners of the page with distinct notes of cinnamon, orange glaze, and a sticky something that felt like dried egg yolk. Nico grinned, wiped his hands on his pants, and went to move Gus off of Brant's chest and into his crate.

CHAPTER 9

Friday 1:15 pm

Nico had tried to be very quiet while he scooped the disgusting pile of undigested bird bones and feathers from the corner of the basement, but he didn't really need to be; Remi had slept like the dead. Brant was also out like a busted lightbulb, having rolled onto his side on the couch. Nico had thoughtfully pulled the blackout curtains closed in the living room so Brant didn't have to be disturbed by the rare for this time of year but still obnoxiously cheerful, morning sun. He perused the small bookshelf in the guest room and found a fascinating book called Nanny Ogg's Cookbook. Just after noon, he kept himself busy by putting together a big brunch for the both of them. Nico was opting not to think too hard about how Remi would find sustenance.

Brant awoke just after 1 pm and was dragging himself to the bathroom when he saw Nico in the kitchen. He raised his eyebrows at him in a clear sign of, "How did it go?" while Nico nodded back an "all good". Nico went down to check on Gus and Remi again and they were both still fast asleep. Sometime in the last hour, Gus had awoken and crawled from his crate to sleep curled up next to Remi which was honestly such an endearing sight.

Nico was still absorbed in the cookbook when Brant appeared from a fresh shower, both hands full, a coffee mug in one and a warm brunch plate in the other. He nodded his thanks and Nico nodded back. The fact that they had developed a shorthand so quickly made Nico smile at the thought.

"What's so funny?" Brant said, still groggy from sleep.

"Nothing," said Nico. "Couldn't make out all of your note. Did it say you talked to your contact again?"

"Yeah. He thinks we should try The Golden Knight. It's a dance club not far from where we were last night, actually. 10th and Fernside. Fancy place. We just need to wait for..." Brant trailed off as he looked towards the basement.

"Yeah, no problem," Nico said to take his mind off it. "I'm glad you two sorted things out. And yeah, those treats were just deadly!" Nico held his hands up in prayer. "Seriously. Where did you come up with the savory cookie thing?"

Brant looked down at his rapidly emptying plate. "Yeah, that was Remi's idea," he said, his voice muffled behind the food. "They aren't bad. He's a surprisingly good cook for someone who doesn't eat." Brant looked sheepish, so Nico didn't press him further about it. "Cool," Nico replied. "Well, they are both still out. You want to play a video game?"

"Yeah, I got some good ones," said Brant, who needed some time to think over their game plan for the night. He took his cleaned-off plate to the kitchen, dropped it in the dishwasher, and joined his new friend for a few hours in some low-stakes entertainment.

A good five hours had passed pleasantly for Nico and Brant as they waited for the other two to rise at sunset. They had lost themselves in the joy of the epic battle between horse-mounted Riders of Ohan and the bloodthirsty orcs in the epic fantasy video game. Nico realized with a shock that the very creatures he was battling in the game might really exist. What if he met an orc in downtown? Or at the garden center? Did orcs grow plants? The presence of Gus in his immediate life made him rethink the way that the magical realm diverged from the tales and games he'd always played. Nico drew his attention to the sounds of Remi ascending the basement.

The vampire was holding Gustopher tenderly, the babe's eyes opening slowly and blinking a few times to register his surroundings.

Brant set down the recipe book he was reviewing and stood.

"I think it's time we had that talk," Brant said darkly.

Remi nodded his assent, handing the gargoyle over to Nico. Gustopher shifted slightly so he could look up at Nico, reaching up a claw to pat his face. Nico's heart melted entirely. He was focused on Gus's entrancing gaze when Remi spoke.

"Do you see his attachment to you, young gardener? His protection of you is already quite strong," Remi said softly. He watched them both for a moment but turned to Brant.

"I will assure you again, Mimolette, I am not a danger to you or the little one. Whether danger may follow me, however," he shrugged as if he recognized this could be a possibility, pushing out his lips slightly, "this I cannot say."

Brant's face clouded but he said nothing, gesturing to Remi to continue. Gus was watching the conversation now, his ears perked up slightly.

"There are *some* things I am at liberty to share, though I find it is more fun not to. But on the opposite hand, both of you are breathtakingly ignorant, and in this way, you could get killed or worse, leave l'enfant without his bounty."

Brant began to interrupt, but Remi forestalled him with a hand raised in the air. "Here is what I offer in faith, and here is what I know." Remi paused slightly. Clearly, sharing confidences was not in his comfort zone.

"What I know is that the other vampires are a bit...how do you say it, peeved with me that I have stopped taking blood from humans. It is this, along with the fact that I destroyed a few of them about five years ago for trying to kill some humans that meant a great deal to me." The emotions crossing his face were complicated; there was fury, regret, and what looked like love briefly, followed by determination. "I have been in hiding in Wisconsin as you astutely observed."

Brant's expression had turned to surprise. "They've been hunting you this whole time?"

Remi nodded grimly. "Vampires do not sanction humans knowing much of our ways, but grudges are held for a long, long time as reckoned by your kind. They could hunt me for 40 years and it would be a short commercial break, as you would say," he smiled faintly, attempting to lighten the mood. Nico's heart tightened at the idea of his friend being treated as an outsider. He knew that feeling all too well.

Remi continued, "I know you are concerned with Gustopher's safety, and if you both believe I would hinder your attempts to find his owner, of course, I will leave immediately. There is always the danger that I will be found by the Camorra." He looked at Gus now, as if taking in the sight of him for the last time, "But should you allow me to stay, I can offer my abilities to continue the search for Rubra."

Nico cut in, "What is the Camorra?"

Remi looked uncomfortable again and said only, "It is what passes for vampire governance. It's more like a tribunal," he said, disdain dripping from the words. He stood abruptly and walked to the doorframe of the living room, leaning against it and looking into the kitchen.

Brant and Nico looked at each other, gauging the credibility of Remi's story in each others' eyes. Nico clearly still trusted Remi but that was Nico's way. Brant believed him but noticed that Remi had left something out, which was *his* way.

"All right. That's valuable intel. Now, why don't you tell me something in good faith." Brant said in response, emphasizing the second half of what Remi agreed to share.

Remi turned back to face all three of them, his face back to its sunny, impish look.

"Oh, that's easy. Didn't you wonder why we've all been spilling our secrets to each other?" As Brant started to rise, Remi dropped the rest of his bombshell, "Gus's persuasive magic is working on all of us."

CHAPTER 10

Brant was in a bit of a temper. He was stewing in his thoughts after the conversation with Remi. He'd gone to his room to take a moment to absorb what he had just learned. *Finally something makes sense about this whole drama,* thought Brant. The vampire had explained — taking entirely too much pleasure in it — that Gus had a kind of magic that *nudged* people around him to divulge their innermost hearts. At least, Remi had implied that of the gargoyles he knew, this was a magic they could cast around them. Remi didn't expound on how he knew this, whether it applied to all gargoyles, how many gargoyles he had met before, or anything else of usefulness.

Brant felt a bit, well, manipulated. He had clocked that personal details had been shared quite quickly even among guys that liked each other, but he didn't like the idea of an outside force pushing him that way. He presumed that Nico was just as uneasy. It certainly cleared up a few things that had happened along the way, too. And Brant did like having the information. He was especially relieved that Remi had also come clean that he was a fugitive. Getting involved in vampire politics was *not* on his radar for the evening, but he reasoned that the risk was only for a day or two and there'd been no signs that the vampires who were looking for Remi were close enough for himself or Nico to get caught in the crossfire.

Brant had pressed Remi for more details about Gus and his kind, but Remi had only twirled away and shut himself in the basement, snickering and refusing to elaborate. Clearly, the inclination to share details could be resisted. Remi was proof of that.

Brant had finally calmed down when he emerged from his bedroom and shared a look of exasperation with Nico. Nico gave him a look that conveyed the entire idiom, "In for a penny, in for a pound." Nico had merely shrugged his shoulders, reminding Brant that they had all had free will and that if they really were not willing to make sure Gustopher was in good hands, they would've handed him over to the security guards at the bar last night and just walked away.

Before they left the house, Brant strapped Gus into Nico's car. They decided that if they were to find Rubra at their next stop, it would be best to hand Gus over straightaway. The longer Brant knew the kid, the more he didn't want to do that, whether he was swayed by magic or not, but he was beginning to feel the difference between the pull of the protective magic and his desire to do the right thing. It was like hearing a distant noise and guessing what it was, and actually finding the source. Once you were able to identify the sound, the different notes made more sense. He wasn't sure if he was ready for all the surprises that Gus seemed to have in store, and the adventure aspect was beginning to wear off. He just wanted the little dude to have the best life possible. Gus grinned his lolling tongue at his caretakers from the backseat. His low, guttural noises were rising and falling like he was playing a game of vocal teeter-totter.

Nico drove through the city streets and back across the Fernside Bridge with Brant giving the occasional direction from the back. Remi was up front, looking refreshed. They had all discussed a game plan on the drive over. Nico was the calmer head, but Brant was able to read the social cues of any given situation a bit better. And Remi had his super-speed and hearing as well as strength should a conflict come up. This time they elected to take the sneakier route; get into the club, split up, and scope out the place to see if they could avoid getting turned away by Rubra's men before finding the crime boss.

As they pulled up a few streets away in front of a dumpling restaurant, the guys all turned to face each other. Nico spoke first.

"Okay, we've decided to do things differently this time. We are all going in together, but when we get in, we are splitting up. Make friends, be charming. The goal is to be inconspicuous so we can see if Rubra is here." Nico was pulling out some tools from various pockets as he spoke.

"Who are you, Sam Gamgee?" Brant teased.

Nico grinned back and said in mock defense, "These are clippers! I keep bonsais of my own, and there's no way they will let me walk in there with a bladed object. I forgot they were in my pants."

Remi leaned in, speaking with quiet sincerity, "I met Merry and Pippin once. They're real."

Remi broke into a huge grin, and even with his fangs, giggled. In the short time they had known him, they could count on one thing: Remi was allergic to being serious. It was sort of endearing once you got past the vampire thing. And the roller skating thing. And the cheese thing.

Nico shook his head. "Anyway. Remi, if you learn something we should know, just give us some sort of signal and we can convene."

"A SIGNAL. Oh, this is so exciting. Should I dance again?" He wiggled his hips in his seat experimentally.

"Maybe don't choreograph something right now," Brant said, drolly. "Nico means find something subtle we can understand. Since it will be loud, let's use a hand gesture." He held up his hand with an open palm, and closed it deliberately, folding his fingers down but leaving the thumb extended and repeated the motion 3 times. It looked like a really stiff wave you would give someone across a crowded room.

Everyone attempted the motion and nodded their agreement.

Gustopher had fallen asleep again on the drive over, so Nico extracted the baby carrier from the trunk and quietly lifted him into the wrap, giving him a gentle kiss and rubbing his claws softly before shutting the car doors with meticulous care.

They approached the club entrance and saw a line of about 50 patrons wearing their sexiest clothes and shifting about in the chilly air impatiently. A sign glowed overhead with yellow lettering that read the name "The Golden Knight" accompanied by a minimalistic design of an Italian medieval close-helmet at the end of the banner.

Nico and Brant looked uncomfortably at their jeans and t-shirts, while Remi smiled smugly at his crisp, tailored slacks and jacket. He reassured them that they were getting in, no problem.

"Oh, are you going to hypnotize them?" Brant asked excitedly, keeping his voice low.

"Of course not. I am going to persuade them." He waggled his eyebrows at a nearby security camera. Nico and Brant caught the hint, even though they could barely make out the shadow outline of the camera from such a far distance.

As they approached the bouncer, Brant and Remi stood taller, puffing out both their chests and throwing back their shoulders. Nico followed suit.

Remi spoke first to the security guard, a massive Black man who towered over them at an impressive 6'6. He was rolling muscle and the towering confidence that he not only was the checkpoint, but he was also the road itself. He was wearing a melted-to-his-body, exquisitely cut red blazer over a white button-down shirt with huge rainbow-colored polka dots on it, stretched taut over his chest complete with matching red tailored slacks and walnut-colored brown loafers. When he spoke, it was like a classical music radio DJ was slowly waking up a Sunday morning audience at 9 am.

"Just you three fine gentlemen, and the...little one, is it?" He poured out the words like oil in a pan.

Remi was so charmed by the guard that he momentarily faltered.

"Oui, it is four of us who wish to patronize your fine establishment and we will be on our best behavior, which for me, is love, not war." He smiled in his goofy manner. The guard was not fooled. He frowned at Remi and waved him aside. He gestured Nico forward. Remi looked hurt but stepped to the left. Nervously, Nico stepped up and was so close he could smell the spice on the man's breath. Without thinking he said, "Did you have extra cinnamon on your latte?"

The guard looked startled, then let out a chuckle that broke in low waves like a muffler being revved in a street race.

"Now, how did you know that?" he asked lightly.

"I can smell it and guessed you had coffee before starting your shift. These guys are all right. I can promise you they aren't interested in making a scene. Just need a break from the family reunion. The kids were a terror." Nico lied smoothly. "This one is too precious to be left with my family." Nico rolled his eyes while gesturing at the back of Gus's head covered in a blanket, as if exasperated with this imaginary and impossible clan. Although given the current climate at home, he did consider his family a bit impossible.

Brant's eyes shot up, impressed, and Remi affected the look of a tired uncle after a long day of patient suffering. He hadn't seen daylight in several centuries but the reminder of the terror of children brought a convincing weariness to his eyes.

The bouncer's eyes lit up. "I got about 12 nieces and nephews that I would hang the moon for, but even my muscles can barely keep up." He laughed so deeply that the crowd looked to the sky for thunder.

"Come on in and have a great time. That little one will need to be out of here before 11 p.m., though, " he gestured to the three, waving them in.

Brant turned to Nico. "Nice work."

"Thanks. Okay. I will take the main bar; you take the back patio; we can leave Remi the dance floor," Nico smirked. Brant grinned back at him.

"That ought to draw some comments."

CHAPTER 11

Friday 8 pm

Nico watched the two men separate from their motley brat pack and head off in opposite directions across the club. He took in the surroundings briefly, as it helped his anxiety calm, just slightly. Settings like this were peak stress for a man like him, as there were a million social cues that needed to be interpreted, and fast. Throw in alcohol and it made the stakes even higher.

Nico's relief at the guys' acceptance had vanished, and he wished that he could just wingman alongside them and shadow their casual confidence. Interacting with women was less of a threat than interacting with other men. And as much as Nico would've tried his hand at flirting with the women there, he needed to stay focused.

He didn't love the idea of trying to approach people at the main bar, but since he was the one that faded into the woodwork more, he figured he could eavesdrop on conversations and listen for staff and security who might give a clue to Rubra's whereabouts if he was here somewhere. He could see a few hallways leading off to other rooms and figured Brant and Remi would explore those.

As Nico pivoted to take in the main area, he scanned the various alcoves looking for visiting political powerheads, athletic stars, musicians, and other peacocks of the upper-crust world. He figured that if Rubra was there, he would be hobnobbing with other powerful people of influence.

The dance club boasted an atmosphere of elegant but stark design. It was an enormous rectangular room with a black, glittery dance floor and no windows showing to the outside. There were a few skylights, and though the moon was not out, Nico could picture how lovely the light would fall through the ceiling at just the right angle. The ceiling edges were lined with blue and yellow neon lighting, presumably to go with the theme of the neon sign out front.

The booths lining the wall of the main dance floor were warm and inviting in dark blue velvet with yellow accents, promising a place to rest from the dancing. The waitstaff hovered around these booths, the empty glasses they collected clinking against each other on their trays. The art above them was in gilded frames and had portraits of royalty and famous figureheads throughout history. It gave the booths the feeling of a private portrait hall.

Nico parked himself and Gustopher — who was still sleeping soundly in the baby carrier, his head lolled to one side — near the corner of the C-shaped bar, which was a shiny, obsidian black on top and had matching golden neon lighting underneath it to match the rest of the room. The bar was built to handle over 100 people at once, with stations for bar backs, wait staff, and security. Two long sets of clear glass shelves were mounted on the wall behind it with a frosted glass wall behind the shelves adorned with embossed floral leaves and vines. Another enormous golden knight neon sign glowed from between the shelves on the center of the wall behind the bottles.

As Nico turned back, scanning the dance floor, he saw the usual groups of people — about 30 couples sprinkled here and there. A few were skilled dancers, but most were just enjoying the music. A bachelorette party was weaving about precariously with tinsel crowns, sashes, and penis-shaped candy rings. They all had Pez candy dispensers that Nico suspected were not dispensing sweets. The ladies were laughing and raising their voices over the music, clearly enjoying themselves. Nico was surprised to see Remi in the middle among these women, having the time of his life cutting loose and dancing with every one of them, his eyes closed in rapture as if he were hearing from angels directly. He managed to turn kissing hands into an R-rated display. He had either forgotten why they were there or had already finished his loop of the dance floor. Nico watched Remi's ease with the ladies with wistful envy.

On the other side of Remi and across the dance floor, he noticed a group of people that had taken over two large seating areas meant to fit 10 people apiece. They looked like athletes, given that they were wearing jerseys. He couldn't see well enough from this distance, so he squinted to get a better look.

He could clearly pick out what looked like hockey players as they were the boisterous young men, gesticulating and expressive with their body language, sloshing beers and pointing at each other, making jokes. Nico envied the ease in their collective masculinity, all bodily trust and brotherhood. They draped their arms around each others' necks and leaned on each other. They touched with familiarity and intimacy. The friendships radiated like a heat wave.

As Nico studied the group of them searching for any sign of Rubra, two elements stood out among the players; one was an enormous trophy in the center of one of the booth tables. It stood at almost three feet tall and was made entirely of silver, with a cylindrical wide barrel base and ascending tiers leading up to a wide-brimmed bowl on top, starkly resembling a widowed aunt's punch bowl served at a summertime tea party.

Besides the impressive trophy, the second thing that stood out was an older white gentleman in his late 50s, with both a deeply bemused and resigned look on his face. He looked like a beloved uncle chaperon and he scanned the room constantly, his eyes always being drawn back to the trophy. He wore a blazer over a white shirt. He made eye contact with Nico and after a long stare, nodded a greeting in return. Nico smiled nervously and nodded back.

Brant approached Nico from the back door leading out to the patio.

"Any luck?" Nico asked.

"None for me, the back patio is nice, just boring. Massive, too," Brant said dismissively. He saw Nico's gaze across the dance floor and mistook it for his eyeing the women. "Did you want to talk to...the ladies?" Brant asked, encouraging, eyebrows waggling.

Nico gave Brant a look of uncertainty.

"Oh-ho! So you do want to talk to them? I could be your wingman!" Brant said excitedly. "I'm an excellent wingman."

"Raincheck on the wingmanning, or is it wingmann'd? Anyway. I think we should talk to these hockey players and that trophy guard. I don't see anyone who fits Rubra's description, but because he's such a sports nut, they have to be meeting up with this team at some point, right?" Nico reasoned.

"Wow, fantastic work!" Brant looked impressed. "Wait. Did you say hockey players?" Brant's voice had grown faint, and Nico looked at him in surprise. Brant had turned and his jaw had dropped. He was already moving towards the booth across the room.

As Nico and Brant drew closer, weaving in and out of the dancing throng, the trophy guard made eye contact with both of them this time. His eyes lingered on the baby carrier which partially shrouded Gus's features but even in the dim light, the ears could be distinguished, poking out from the sides at an angle.

As they were making their way over, Brant elbowed Nico in the ribs. Brant hadn't even seen Remi, he walked almost right past him. He only had eyes for the trophy.

"Is that THE MANLEY CUP?!" he shouted, both in excitement and to carry his voice over the music.

"I have no idea. Is it?" Nico asked.

"Dude. Duuuuuuuddddde. This is epic. This is super important for you to know. The Manley Cup is over 120 years old! It was donated by Lord Manley of Weston, son of the Earl of Herby. It is the biggest prize given to the winning hockey team and they get to have it for an entire year. Usually, the Cup travels around with different players for a few months before it goes on its *own touring schedule*. I can't believe I didn't see it at first. I just didn't expect it, HERE." Brant was almost breathless and his feet became very bouncy as he moved forward and back in anguished excitement. Nico held back a laugh.

"Okay, well, we have a good excuse to talk to them, then. Besides Gus." Nico said, nudging the indecisive Brant deeper in the direction of the velvet booths and the hockey players.

The teammates had noticed the oddball pair at this point, and they were already wearing the expressions that well-known people get when they know they are about to be approached by die-hard fans. But the trophy guard continued to smile his open, friendly grin like the three of them were in on some secret.

Nico and Brant had finally reached the booth, and Brant's hand began to unconsciously rise to touch it. The hockey players laughed good-naturedly, all nodding their understanding of his awe. Nico reached out and slowly lowered Brant's hand because his eyes were completely fixed on the Cup itself.

"Not without permission, Brant," Nico said, loud enough for everyone to hear.

The table broke into roaring laughter, but it was the welcoming kind, the brotherly kind.

"May I please touch the Manley Cup? This is the honor of a lifetime. " Brant asked reverently, his eyes pleading with the trophy guard.

"You may touch it, but not lift it. Selfies are permitted. Nothing R-rated in the picture or with your hands, please." The guard spoke the well-rehearsed words easily, his voice both commanding and friendly. His authoritative and kind demeanor was clearly well-respected.

As Brant was basking in the glory of the Manley Cup, Nico gestured to the trophy guard if he and Gus could sit down. The man nodded for the two of them to sit and as Nico settled into the booth, the guard could clearly see Gustopher's face. He startled for a second and let out a sound of disbelief.

"Is that a gargoyle? Wow, I travel the wide world and I thought I had seen everything," he marveled. Gus opened his eyes sleepily and blinked several times. His ears began to wiggle and Nico could see the older man melt completely. His formerly alert manner had short-circuited and he watched Gus in abject fascination.

Gus reached out one of his claws and the man took it, shaking it in a tiny handshake.

"I'm Jasper, you absolute joy of creation. What's your name?" Jasper said.

"His name is Gustopher but he doesn't talk much. We found him left behind and are trying to find his owner, who we think is here. Not just here, but owns this bar." Nico heard the words coming out of his mouth and despite knowing that it was Gus's magic that made him divulge this private detail, he was still surprised when it happened. He recovered and said, "Viscidius Rubra? Have you heard of him?" Nico asked, hopeful.

"Oh, yes. Mr. Rubra is a big hockey fan, obviously. He extended a personal invitation for us to come and visit his establishments. And while the offer was generous, it's not the only reason why we came. The main reason is that this is the hometown of one of the winning players, Patrice," Jasper pointed across the booth, a strong young man in his early 30s with tanned skin, a square jaw, a crooked nose that had clearly been broken several times, and kind brown eyes. Patrice was quietly listening to his friend's boasting but caught Nico's glance, raising his beer slightly. Jasper continued, "He wanted to come here and celebrate his one day at his favorite dance club." Nico tipped his chin forward and up in greeting like he had learned from Brant.

"Patrice!" Someone shouted, and the man Nico had been looking at turned away.

Brant was still taking pictures with the Cup and the hockey players who were conversing with him easily. Brant had that way about him. Extroverts.

Nico's attention returned to the conversation. "His one day?" he repeated.

"Yes, the winning team gets 100 days to celebrate how they wish with the Cup. They usually break up the days amongst themselves and for the next two days, I'm in town to accompany it here along with these five rascals." Jasper smiled as he spoke, clearly a man who enjoyed his work.

"Wow. That's incredible. I forgot to say, but my name is Nico. I guard bonsai trees at the botanical garden, and that goofball over there is Brant. He is an incredible baker." This was bolder than Nico usually shared upon a first meeting, but Jasper felt like a kindred spirit. Besides, Gus liked him and still hadn't let go of Jasper's fingers.

"Good golly, Ms. Molly, that's quite a pairing. How did you two meet?" Jasper replied, curiosity causing him to lean in closer. As Nico told the story of how the circumstances started the night before, Jasper shook with delight and astonishment.

"You are on an adventure, and make no mistake, I don't think you are going to find what you need here, and I sorely wish I could accompany you, but my duty is to stay with the Cup at all times."

"At all times? Don't you get time off?" Nico couldn't imagine his introverted self having no privacy or quiet. The gardens were so necessary for his peace of mind. He could never leave them.

"Well, there's four of us total, and there's usually two of us during the 100-day tour, then the Cup itself has a list of cities it visits. So I do work long days and travel extensively, yes."

"Wow. Well, I'm so glad I got to meet you, Jasper. All of us; Brant, Gus, and myself." Nico reached out to shake his hand, practicing his reach.

Jasper grasped his hand and shook it firmly several times. "Nice to meet you too. I hope you find Mr. Rubra. Although I have to tell you, I can't imagine that little guy with anyone else, just for the record," he added with admiration. Nico's throat had gone tight so he only nodded back.

"It's natural to care about him. After all, you rescued the little tyke. And no one knows what lies next. You remember that, son." Jasper winked at Nico and Nico smiled back at him.

Nico turned away from Jasper and started to head over to Brant, who was still bonding with the hockey players. Gus reached out his hand and pouted as they left Jasper, making fidgety noises, and the trophy guard shook his head, smiling ruefully.

As he approached Brant he wondered, as he constantly did, if his passing would be successful in such a large group of men. Counting the players, Nico could see half a dozen admirers, but still. Passing among one or two men usually wasn't an issue, and certainly Brant made it clear that he would stand with him should a conflict come up, but a large group of young men in this setting made the hairs on the back of Nico's neck stand up. He tried to appear relaxed and jiggled Gustopher in an effort to shake off some nerves.

But Nico's worries were for nothing because as he approached Brant, Gus reached out his claws in the "uppy" gesture that is universally understood by all adults in the known and unknown universe to mean "hold me." As soon as Brant took Gustopher into his arms, the entire group lost their minds. Half of them folded over in abject joy, unable to contain themselves, pounding their fists, creating a drum beat with shaking glasses as percussion. When they raised their heads, joyful tears were clearly being wiped from their eyes. A few others who were standing nearby had collapsed on their fellow teammates' shoulders, making noises like a baby harp seal, squealing in delight.

The last two had grown completely blank expressions, their eyes as wide as seedling pots, with their mouths opening and closing like a strong breeze fluttering a fabric curtain. Gus's magic had taken hold instantaneously. A thought popped into Nico's head: *Is his magic growing stronger around more people?*

"So, Brant, the baby is feeling restless. I think we should plan our next move." Nico said conversationally, savoring the distraction.

Brant nodded his agreement. "These guys know of Rubra but they don't know where to find him. How did you do?"

"Basically the same. But we did make a new friend." Nico gestured to Jasper, who was still in the booth. Jasper waved at Gus, and Gus waved back both his claws furiously, reaching for Jasper again. Brant chuckled in response and raised a hand to wave back.

Remi, who had been on the dance floor the entire time, was there in an instant. "Was that ze secret wave? Did you find something out? Where is ze big bad man?"

"Remi, it's okay. We didn't find the owner. Gus recruited a whole team of protectors, though. How did you do?" Nico said soothingly.

"Oh! Yes, I heard everything we needed from the manager in the back office over 30 minutes ago. Monsieur Rubra is not here; he is at his casino outside of town this evening." Remi smiled in his mischievous manner, turning to wave at the bachelorettes on the dance floor. They all jumped up and down and crooned at him lovingly.

"Wait, you had the information we needed 30 minutes ago?! Why didn't you tell us?" Brant asked, his temper flaring again. Nico could see that he was still resenting the conversation earlier and Remi's blatant refusal to share what he knew.

Brant was shouting now, "What is with you, man? You just do shit in your own time and your own way, I guess, and just...screw everyone else?"

While the music continued pounding from the speakers near the DJ booth, the table had gone still. Nico could feel the shift in Remi, that razor's edge that he liked to toy with, provoking people and then deciding if he wanted to play along or have a fight. It wasn't what you'd call a healthy habit.

Remi's eyes sparkled at the escalation, and he said, "You sweet block of Brie, I told you. I am on VACATION. I am accompanying you, yes, but I'm going to *enjoy myself*. Besides, Gus needed the socializing and you all made *such* nice friends." He said gleefully, nodding at his logic. He clearly had chosen playful over killer, at least in this instance.

Brant eyed Remi suspiciously. "I'm so sick of your games. What else haven't you been telling us, Remi?"

"Oh, la la, dee dee dee! Now you are beginning to understand! How delightful you have finally caught up!" Remi was positively bouncing with delight, clapping his hands. "Yes, it is true. I carry many secrets from my long life, but why would I spill them all to you, who I have just met, oui? A mere babe in arms, and one with no sense of humor? What a foolish move on my part, indeed!" His eyes flashed for just a moment in the dark, and Nico could tell that though Remi was playing his amusement for the gathered people, his irritation was plain. And growing.

Remi leaned down but managed to pitch his voice so everyone nearby could hear, "Make no mistake, young Brant. It is my interest in this babe and *what he will do next* that compels me. I have not gotten to the age I am by trusting every person who crosses my path." Remi bristled dangerously.

Jasper had risen during this interaction, his back to the players who had returned to their drinks but were deep in whispered conversation, watching the entire exchange.

"If you will permit me? I have some experience with resolving conflicts." He addressed all three of them, his hand touching Gus briefly on the claw. Gus closed his eyes, soothed. Remi waved his assent with a hand. "I understand perfectly what you mean," Jasper said, diplomatic and soothing. "You have been helping them to find Mr. Rubra and now they are showing ingratitude with mistrust. Is that right? You must care a great deal for the bantling." Jasper said with great respect, lowering his head slightly.

Remi softened instantly, "Bantling. I haven't heard that word in a long time." He cocked his head, studying Jasper more closely. "I have missed such words. They bring such color to the conversation," he sighed wistfully.

"My great-grandmother called me that when I was very young," Jasper said with reverence.

Jasper and Remi studied each other for a moment, and without another word, clasped forearms and shook firmly. Nico studied this exchange with interest, trying to glean what had passed between them. Jasper had diffused the rising conflict by finding common ground with the vampire. Nico was deeply grateful to Jasper at that moment because, by the time he would've figured out exactly what was wrong, the other two might've been at blows already.

Unfortunately, though, the argument had caught the attention of the security staff. A group of six guards had approached the booth, looking hostile as jagged metal. Nico recognized one of the men from the bar the night before. All of the approaching guards wore expressions of deadly malice, but their leader wore the face of someone who particularly enjoyed cruelty.

The one that Nico recognized addressed Brant, almost spitting the words, "You don't know when to leave well enough alone, do you? It's bad enough that your boss V sent you last night to taunt Rubra with your blackmail, but now you show up with the...thing you are blackmailing him for? What kind of an idiot does that? Either you are that stupid or that ballsy. I don't really care which. I just want you gone until my boss makes a decision as to how he's going to kill you. I hope it's slow." A dark, satisfied smile had crept into his menacing voice. He paused, calculating. "On the other hand, Rubra would be pretty happy with me if I showed up with this freak for his zoo so wouldn't have to deal with The Volcano at all."

Brant realized the misunderstanding and started to speak but Remi cut him off with a raised hand, already re-directing his unspent anger at the sadist.

"Oh? Do you think you can take the little bantling from us?" He asked the question almost offhand as if he were discussing traffic, all the while pretending to inspect his fingernails. Brant didn't like where this was going. Things were going to get out of hand, and fast. There was Gus to think of, the innocents trying to enjoy themselves, and the players. He couldn't risk any of them, not to mention the prized Manley Cup. He locked eyes with Jasper who understood him in an instant. Jasper began moving the Cup slowly and surreptitiously out of range of the stand-off. The hockey players, however, seemed ready for a brawl and they stood away from the wall, dropping their drinks and fanning out, each one squaring off with an opponent to block the coming offense.

Nico had started to step back from the exchange, shielding Gus with his hands, but club security guards began to flank him. At this moment, several things happened at once.

Brant began shouting to the leader that they didn't work for The Volcano, but the man just shook his head with a snarl of disbelief. He grabbed Remi's lapel, pulled the vampire closer, and started to bring back his arm to hit him. This was, of course, a major miscalculation. Faster than sight, Remi had followed through with the momentum of being pulled forward, tucking his head into the man's chest and rolling into a crouched somersault. Remi's attacker lay on the ground, wheezing from having the wind knocked out of him.

The hockey players had begun grappling maneuvers with the other security guards, either shoving them further from the booth or pushing them away from Gus and Nico. Brant was still shouting at the man on the floor, but by this point, their tall Black friend from outside had come in and was restraining Brant. Jasper had scooped up the Cup and bolted for the exit.

Nico began to run as well, which was a struggle as Gus was keening a pitched wail at Brant and Remi, his arms reaching for them. Nico couldn't tell if the gargoyle was scared or delighted. As he headed for the exit, he looked back over his shoulder. He could see Remi perched on the man's chest now. The leader was still wheezing from first having the breath knocked out of him, and now having Remi sitting on his lungs. Remi had grabbed his head on both sides, clearly about to snap the man's neck, his face a mask of perfect serenity. Nico shouted, "NOOO!" as loud as he could and Remi turned to him, his hands frozen, then slowly removed them from the man's head.

Remi heard a distant sound coming from Nico, so he hesitated, as he knew his little sapling friend would never shout at him unless it was important. He dropped his hands momentarily — he knew this man had to die, the predator in him recognized the worst of humanity — and raised his eyes to find Nico but instead, locked on Gustopher. Remi didn't register anything at that moment — not the room, not Nico, his gentle friend, or Brant, his prickly friend who had seen too much of the world. He gazed into the eyes of his strange and wonderful superior, his both very, very old friend/new friend in a new form, and just stopped fighting. He could feel Gus's magic reach out like ropes, binding him in love, holding his massive vampire strength vertically, like redirecting a busted water pipe. He relaxed and let go of the pounding roar of fury in his soul, and went limp as a handkerchief when the beautiful bouncer from outside lifted him bodily, throwing him, Brant, and just giving Nico a little shove out the door and back into the chilly night.

CHAPTER 12

Friday 9:30 pm

It was a quiet walk to the car, though Gus was squirmy the whole way. Nico was struggling to keep him snug in the carrier and bounced the baby up and down as he walked toward the back passenger door. Nico finally turned to face Remi.

"Were you really going to kill that guy?" Nico blurted out. Gus ceased moving around.

Remi grew thoughtful and considered the question. When he spoke, acres of regret tinged his voice, "It takes a long time to control blood lust. I've only been practicing for a few years. But it wasn't about that. That man had true cruelty in him; I could smell it," Remi finished, his lip curling in remembrance.

Nico wasn't convinced. He was starting to think that Brant had been right; Remi was too dangerous to have around. *Whatever help he brought was negated by the drama and the dangling secrets. And that was going to be double until they untangled the mess of what he'd heard. Did Rubra think they worked for The Volcano? How could they have gotten that impression? How were they going to handle Rubra after this? Was The Volcano coming after them to take Gus as well?* Nico's temples began to pound with stress and anxiety. He wasn't cut out for this. He glanced at Brant, who was

91

studying the ground, deep in thought. Brant hadn't said a word since they were thrown out of the club.

Just then, a commotion down the street made all three men look up. Clearly visible among the huddle of hockey players were Jasper and the Manley Cup, bobbing up and down and heading straight towards them.

As Remi stood a few paces away, Nico and Brant met the group of men in the middle of the sidewalk. Jasper was beaming and said simply, "We would like to accompany you. If that's okay."

Nico and Brant were exchanging a look, trying to decide if this would help or hinder them when the baby let out what can only be described as a lizard roar. He was reaching through the open door, his eyes locked on Jasper. Jasper brought the Cup over and set it down gently next to the SUV. He reached out to pet Gustopher's head, who immediately calmed at his touch. Every man present sighed with relief.

Brant replied without a trace of irony, "As his Majesty demands." He smiled as everyone did mocking bows to Gus, who happily clutched Jasper's hand and burbled his delight.

Brant waved all the players closer. "Listen, couple of things. First off, and we just found this out," he didn't look in Remi's direction, but his face was turned slightly towards the vampire, "but Gus has a bit of...influence that might be working on you guys. Makes you extra chatty. So just give it a second thought if you really want to come with us." He paused to see if anyone had questions, but no one spoke. Brant continued, "The bigger problem is now apparently Viscidius and his men think we work for..." he hesitated, clearly uncertain how much he should share, "someone else. We need to get Gus back to Rubra before anyone gets hurt." He did look at Remi now, and his expression was grim.

"We should head straight to Rubra."

Remi stepped forward to share what he had learned at the club, that Rubra was spending the evening at his casino on the outskirts of town called The Kraken's Den. All trace of teasing and cryptic riddles was gone. While the players were discussing how far away the Kraken's Den was, Nico pulled Brant aside.

"How bad is it?"

"It's not great."

"Can we do this without him?"

"We could try, but I don't like our odds, given what just happened."

Nico sighed. "I don't know how Rubra is going to react. I'm not happy about it, but won't it be easier if he came with us, to help?" Nico lowered his voice. "I still think he wants to help."

Brant looked at Nico, then glanced over at Remi, who was standing next to Gus, strapped into the car seat. He looked up at the stars and said a small prayer under his breath.

"Fine. He can come," he said.

Nico went to tell Remi the good news, and Brant went to talk to the hockey players to coordinate the caravan out to the casino. It was located on the outskirts of town so they had a good 90-minute drive ahead.

Back in the privacy of the SUV, Nico's stomach felt like there was a massive river stone in it. Brant's eyes had a cold light. Remi's demeanor had lost all of its mischief. Gus had quieted some but was not asleep, watching all three of them carefully, his eyes considering the collective mood. Despite their shared grief, all three men buckled their safety belts and started the drive to The Kraken's Den.

As they started the drive, Nico's SUV was in the lead, the hockey players took the middle place in the caravan, and Jasper and the Cup were in a separate car at the back.

As they cruised along through the downtown streets, they passed through a mix of office buildings, college housing, theatres, dry cleaners, hotels, and restaurants, crisscrossing the light-rail train tracks that quilted the city streets. As they moved further from the downtown area, they were passing by a small but surprisingly detailed gothic cathedral. The guys had started a low conversation about the rivalry between the two crime lords, so they didn't notice as Gustopher easily released his chest and lap seat belts, propped his butt up on the edge of the car seat, and before anyone could say a word, flapped his tiny wings experimentally before flying straight out the window and soaring up to the roof of the church.

Chapter 13

Nico shouted something incoherent, his heart leaping in his chest as he saw what was happening in the rear-view mirror. Both Brant and Remi looked immediately to the gargoyle's spot, and seeing that Gustopher was gone, they gaped in a panic. Remi — almost predictably — began to laugh, slapping his leg in enjoyment.

Nico instantly pulled over, and he and Brant were out of the car in a flash. The other two cars behind them pulled over immediately, hockey players jumping out and running across the street like a clown car game. Any stranger passing by would've thought there was a flash mob in the street. Cars passing by honked angrily, but the players just laughed and waved as they dodged traffic. They had joined Brant, Nico, and Remi in a matter of moments. Everyone crowded around to Gus's door, and seeing that the window was fully rolled down and the seat belts neatly undone, they looked expectantly at Remi since he was the one in the backseat.

"Ah, oui. I should have mentioned this. This is, how you say, my bad? Gargoyles are highly intelligent from birth. He wanted to leave, and so he left. The buckles were never going to hold him in." Remi grinned as he dropped his new bomb of knowledge.

Brant and Nico stared back at Remi in that This-Would've-Been-Useful-Earlier kind of look that was becoming so commonplace with him. If there was any chance that Gustopher was not going back to Rubra, Nico would've sat Remi down and peppered him with questions about whatever else he was hiding. He now fully sympathized with Brant and his suspicions. As it was, there wasn't the time or opportunity right now, as they HAD to get the baby off that buttress.

Remi joined in as everyone craned back to stare up at the sharp pinnacles, the steep rooftops between them, with the nave roof barely visible against the stars.

"Why for the love of biscuits would he fly up there?" Brant wondered aloud.

"Because he sees other kin up there, of course," Remi replied easily. "Can't you see the stone gargoyles up there? When they have been without family for so long, they can choose to hibernate. This is what makes them look like stone." Remi continued his 'Gargoyles 101: Their culture and History' lecture the way all professors do, to a room of people who have no clue what they are talking about.

You could look Remi straight in the face and tell him that living, breathing, clothes-shredding, flying-off-from-car seats gargoyles were *not* an everyday occurrence and he would tell you that you were the one who had experienced a loss of reality.

"It's kind of impressive how fast he got up there," Nico said, finally, trying to process what Remi had shared and their predicament. *So Gus flew up there on his own,* he thought. 'He wanted to leave, so he left,' is what Remi had said. Nico was playing this over and over in his mind. He was beginning to have a profound realization, and the implications were massive. His heart leapt at what this could mean, but he didn't want to give any of the others false hope. He had to confirm if his suspicions were true. Remi could have his fun and games, but this was critical. If he could frame his questions carefully enough for the trickster, it would determine the entire course of Gus's life. Nico was chastising himself for not realizing it earlier.   "Remi, are you saying that Gus has been understanding us this whole time?"

"Oui. Yes, of course. I thought you understood this." Remi said pleasantly.

"And you are also saying that he's been choosing to be fed, sleep with us, play with us?" said Nico, his tone getting more urgent.

Brant leaned into Nico. "What is it? What's going on? We don't have time for 20 questions."

"This is important. Even before we get him down — or if we get him down," he said, considering this new possibility.

The hockey players had grown distracted looking for Gus, who had blended quite expertly into the dark silhouette. They were placing bets on who could climb the fastest to retrieve him. Nico needed to make 100% sure and get Gus down before someone got hurt.

"Don't you see? Gus is not a helpless kid. He comprehends. He follows us, and has been choosing us, over and over. He could've left *at any time*." Nico had grabbed Brant's arm, willing him to get this. "Gus chose us when we 'found' him. We didn't rescue him. He *agreed* to come with us. And right now, he's *refusing* to go back to Viscidius!"

Brant looked like a clap of thunder had just broken over his head. The hockey players had all been listening and were nodding slowly, comprehension dawning across their faces. Remi was looking like a middle school teacher, impatiently waiting for a student to get to the solution of a math problem at the front of the class.

Brant finally spoke.

"We need to ask him, directly, " he said, serious.

"Yes. Exactly." Nico was so relieved, that he slumped a little. "But first, we need to coax him down."

Nico's anxiety was coming in tidal waves and escaping through his mouth. "And when you think about it, the fact that he stayed with us at all." Nico turned to Brant. "Does this mean we are good parents? Because I've been wondering if all this exposure is good for hi —" Brant cut Nico off.

"I'm sure we can have a long discussion on the merits and downfalls of taking a kid to the places we've been taking him, but RIGHT NOW, we have to find out how to get him DOWN HERE." Brant looked pointedly from Nico to the church roof, and back again. His eyebrows couldn't have gone any higher without a commercial aircraft and flight clearance from an air traffic tower.

"Right. Getting him down." Nico ran a hand through his short, black hair. "Here's the thing. This *changes everything*. If he really understands us and could've left at any time, it's not our job to tell him what to do or force him. Our job, as his foster-whatever-parents, is to show him why coming with us is better than what he's doing now. So, we need a way to ask him more than anything else." Nico finished.

Brant and Remi stared at Nico in admiration. Remi nodded once, decisively. Before Brant and Nico said another word, Remi took off, flying straight into the air.

As Remi flew up to the buttress, he saw Gus patting a stone gargoyle on the back, trying to get it to wake up and come alive. Gus was perched next to the statue, cooing under his tongue in a tone Remi hadn't heard him make before. The recent drizzle had made the rooftop shine, and the smell of leaves and copper was not unpleasant as he surveyed the twinkling lights of the city laid out before him. He couldn't see the river, but he could smell it; all cutthroat, rainbow trout, black cottonwood, and willow trees, even from here. He landed softly on his feet, braced against the steep slope by putting out a steadying hand. "Gus, mon petit Pont l'Eveque, won't you come and join your anxious foster papas and enjoy some delicious birds? I know the boys want to ask you a very important question, and we cannot all be up here with you." Remi said in a gentle and inviting tone.

Gus turned and looked at Remi with such a crestfallen expression. It was clear that he thought he had found some kin to bond with. The statue perched at the edge, their face held fast in stone, a snarl of disdain emanating malice, showed no signs of coming to life.

Gus nodded at Remi and blinked twice to show his comprehension, and Remi nodded his understanding in return. Remi understood how taxing verbal communication could be for Gus's kind. He had lived a long life, yes. One of the things he'd learned, and especially the hard way, was that it was rare for supernatural creatures to allow outsiders to see how they behaved in private. Survival was about knowing when to keep certain details hidden, just like everyone else on this adventure. But Gus stood to lose the most, and Remi understood this keenly. All of Remi's efforts up to date had been to protect the humans. They couldn't understand that, at least not to the same degree. They would, eventually.

Gus leaned in and growled something into the stone ear, grasping it tightly. He patted the statue on the back and scratched its back affectionately with his claws. He turned back to Remi and made his pitiful 'uppie' gesture, grinning all the while.

"I respect your efforts to manipulate me, little one. It's a worthwhile skill to have if you are interacting with mortals for any length of time." Remi laughed in admiration and held out his arms.

Back on the ground, Nico and Brant were discussing the question they were going to ask Gus. His answer would determine whether or not they went on to return Gus as planned or to confront the knowledge that they would fight rather than return him. Nico and Brant weren't sure they were ready for the answer, but they agreed that whatever he said, they would honor it. They could see the outline of Remi on the rooftop and some of the movements of their charge. It was agonizing to wait, not knowing what they were talking about, but they knew that Remi would find a way to get him down. They were beginning to concoct a very haphazard Plan B that involved rope and a crane, when, after several dreadful minutes, Remi flew down with Gustopher held gently in his arms.

Brant and Nico both made a fuss over the baby, Nico was touching his head and claws affectionately, whereas Brant just bodily took Gus from Remi and held the little one tightly in his bulging arms, the clear relief from panic mixed with affection written on his face. The hockey players and Jasper were 'awwing' over the reunion, mixed with disappointment that they didn't get to scale a church like Spiderman.

"I'm going to make you some special turkey-flavored biscuits when we get you home —" Brant stopped himself, reality abruptly bursting in as he remembered their next destination.

"It's okay, Brant. We are going to do what's best for Gus, right?" Nico nodded at him, a question in his eyes.

"Yes, of course," Brant replied, but the verve was gone from his tone.

Nico looked closely at Gus. As he gazed into that one silver and one golden eye, he spoke lovingly and so, so quietly. "It seems we underestimated you. You've been having a real laugh this entire time, haven't you?" The smile in Nico's voice was full of love. "Well, I'm glad to know that even if you don't need us, you enjoy our company. And we really do care about you, so much. So if you don't want to go back, you just tell us, and we will find a way to make it work, okay? It's your choice." Nico finished, glancing at Brant and Remi. Both of his friends were nodding in encouragement, their eyes on Gus.

Remi cleared his throat. "It seems like a good time to say that gargoyles struggle with verbal speech. It drains their energy, so they communicate in this way very little."

Brant and Nico both looked appraisingly at Remi. It was an apology, of sorts.

Nico turned back to Gustopher. "Well?"

Gustopher looked at each of them, and reached up, forming his front claw into a single point. He gestured down at the ground and said, gravelly but with certainty, "Gus stay."

Brant walked back around to the passenger car door with Gus still in his arms, wiping his eyes and sniffling loudly, murmuring to Gus under his breath. Nico transferred Gus back into the car seat, his heart bursting with happiness, followed immediately by dread. He forced himself to focus. He was shaking his head in disbelief as he rolled the window back up and turned to the toddler. Remi was wearing a canny expression but was quiet.

So if you wouldn't mind, no antics, okay?" Nico asked, hopefully. Gus nodded his assent, breaking into his signature toothy grin. Nico petted the warm scaly head and climbed into the driver's seat. He turned to Brant, sitting in the front.

"Okay, Mr. Mastermind. Tell me, how we are going to get out of this?"

CHAPTER 14

Friday 10:30 pm-12 am

The hockey players were all committed now, all trace of other entertainment out the window. They had decided that despite whatever influence Gus might be exercising upon them, they wanted to follow the guys back to Brant's house. Brant, Nico, and Remi needed to regroup and find a way to tell the second-most powerful man in the city that he couldn't have his property back. Tell him that Gus wasn't property at all. They needed solutions, and going straight to the casino, unprepared, was not the smart thing to do.

As the caravan pulled onto Brant's street, crowding into every nook and cranny of the house, there were oohs and ahhs as the men made a beeline towards the warming drawer still packed with the morning's sweet treats. The platters were devoured in moments. Gus was back to galivanting around the house since midnight seemed to be the hour he got the zoomies and raced from room to room.

The trio all stepped into Brant's bedroom for a quiet moment to try to figure out how on Earth they were going to go into the literal Kraken's Den and confront Viscidius. The added dimension that Rubra now thought that they had been harboring Gustopher from him, that The Volcano had somehow managed to get Gus, well, that complicated matters. Jasper opened the door a few moments later, and the trio were surprised to see him there.

Jasper sat on the bed where they were meeting and said, "I can't explain it, but Gustopher is very, very important. And this isn't just the magic talking. It's my gut. I want to help. So, how far have you gotten?"

Brant sighed in defeat and said sarcastically, "Well, Remi here thinks our best solution is to have Gus pretend to be dead, and then we can revive him later like some sort of Romeo and Juliet play."

"Oui, I will play Juliet, as I make a very convincing dead person," he said gleefully, laying on the floor in an unnervingly still manner. Nico nudged him with his foot; nothing. Nico also let out a dejected sigh of defeat. Remi was not being very helpful, but at least he was not causing trouble.

"We haven't gotten very far, obviously." Nico frowned, "And poisons or playing dead is, believe it or not, not the worst idea he has had." Nico nudged Remi again, who was steadfastly committed to the bit.

They considered a few more weak options, each one growing more and more unrealistic than the last. When the subject of "move to Atlantis" came up, Brant called it.

"That's it. We need a break, let's go see what the others are up to."

Brant opened the bedroom door just in time to see Gus flying through the air from one side of the house to the other, his little mouth open in joy, landing in the top of the Manley Cup bowl.

Saturday 2:45 am

Brant was a fun-loving guy; he was. He had loved hanging out with his Army buddies; his unit had gotten up to all kinds of antics both in base camp and on tour. He thought of those times as wild, unchecked, and unsupervised pure chaos. He thought he had seen it all, for the most part. But that was before Gus. There was something about the little dude that brought out the mischief in everyone.

For instance, he was witnessing a whole group of guys play Gargoyle Roulette, (invented on the spot, obviously) where the hockey players took a bottle and spun it clockwise on the floor and whoever the bottle landed on, everyone would scatter and Gus would chase his target until he caught them by the leg and wrapped himself around them, squealing. Then there was Toss the Baby, which he had walked in on earlier. The rules to that one seemed self-explanatory enough. But Brant's favorite, despite being the least hygienic, was the game of Tickle the Tummy, where the guys played a song from the radio, tossing his milk frother back and forth from guy to guy, and when the song ended, whoever was holding the milk frother would tickle Gustopher's tummy with the kitchen appliance. He was going to have to buy a new one of those, obviously.

As he watched the guys all lay on their backs (even Jasper!) with their feet in the air, looking like a weird table of soled feet, they passed Gus up one side and down the other, trying not to drop him, with Gus rolled into a tight ball, Brant and Remi stood in the kitchen, enjoying the antics from afar. Nico had gone upstairs to try to get some sleep, as it was the early morning hours, and he had lost his fight with consciousness around 2 am. They had been cooking up new batches of both sweet and savory goods for the guys. Gus looked so happy, his eyes were gleaming, reflected in the various lamps and indirect light of the room.

"I still don't know what we are going to do tomorrow night," Brant said, as he pulled another tray of madeleines from the oven.

Remi said patiently, "Bien sur. I am not sure what we can do. Let the man know that Gus has chosen this life, not one in a cage," as he transferred raspberry shortbread thumbprint cookies to a cooling rack. He liked helping Brant in the kitchen, and it seemed to calm his friend's suspicious nature.

"Couldn't you...I don't know...show your fangs?" Brant said, hesitating. He was clearly frustrated with trying to find a solution where no one got hurt.

Remi looked down, choosing his words carefully. "I can't draw too much attention to myself. Threatening a man such as him would not help my...situation back home."

Brant nodded without looking up, but his face showed an awareness between the lines of what Remi was choosing not to say. He couldn't risk it, and Brant could respect that.

"I guess we'll just take it on the jaw, then," he said. "I hope there's someone left when we are done. To take care of Gus, I mean." He took a deep breath, enjoying the smells of his kitchen. As always, it brought him back to his center.

"Take it on the jaw! Carré Corse, aren't you dramatic!" Remi exclaimed. "I am confident that Gus will take care of us, in the end." He winked at Brant. Brant stared at him, remembering the last 48 hours and the types of games Remi liked to play.

"Wait. REMI. Do you know something else? What do you mean?" Brant said as Remi started walking away. The elevated shouts of the players in the living room showed that a clear winner of the latest game had happened. Brant was shocked they hadn't progressed to piggyback rides. Yet.

But he was already descending the basement stairs, a wave over his shoulder dismissing Brant. "Gus will be fine, I assure you! MORE than fine!" He replied merrily, his voice echoing into the darkness below.

Brant turned back to the living room, surveying the carnage.

"One of you is giving that kid a bath after touching all your stinky feet, and it is NOT going to be me!"

Chapter 15

Saturday 1 pm

Nico awoke to another heavenly smell and breathed in and out several times to fully savor the moment. Wisps of tangy raspberry, the unmistakable velvet notes of chocolate, and a sharp, cheesy smell were all drifting under the door and landing as softly on him as the light but cozy blanket draped across his shoulders. He was struggling to adapt to this new sleep schedule, and if they made it through this, he would have to work out a schedule with Brant. Nico was shocked at how fast he had adapted to the idea of being a parent, but it was a pleasant surprise.

As he made his way out of the guest room, there were telltale signs that the night had been...well, pretty bonkers. The bathroom sink had smears of toothpaste in it, distinctly claw-shaped. There were imprints of soap bubbles dried onto the wallpaper. Wet towels, shredded to rags, were lying defeated on the floor. They looked so pitiful, Nico grabbed them to throw in the trash and give them a decent burial. As he stepped into the living room, it was a mass of sleeping hockey players — was that a blanket fort? — pillow feathers stuck to surfaces, walls, and furniture, and in the middle of it all, curled up with a look of perfect innocence in sleep, was Gustopher. He had at least four guys surrounding him, all legs and arms thrown haphazardly in sleep across cushions and rumpled blankets. Nico shook his head. Should he be surprised at this point? No, he reasoned, he should not. He looked around for Jasper, and found him sitting in the recliner chair in the corner, his hand holding fast to the Manley Cup, even in his sleep. Nico could see Gus's plushie bumblebee poking out the top.

An hour later, all the guys and Gus were beginning to stir. Nico had made as big of a breakfast as he could; the kitchen island was covered in sliced fruit, piles of bacon and sausage, fresh coffee, orange juice, grapefruit juice, hot tea, and of course, all of Brant's signature dishes from the night prior. He made a mental note to chip in a few bucks. Brant had been eaten out of house and home in two days flat.

While all the guys were in the kitchen, Nico carefully walked down the basement stairs with Gus in his arms to leave him with Remi. They could both catch the last few hours of needed rest. As he came back into the kitchen, he nodded at Jasper to follow him to the living room. Jasper's plate was loaded to the brim. Nico smiled, looking at the plate, and said, "Busy night, huh?"

"Very memorable," Jasper agreed, stuffing his mouth with sausage and cinnamon roll in an enormous bite from his fork.

"Did you guys figure out how we are going to tell Viscidius the news?" Nico said, his voice hopeful.

Jasper shook his head no, looking like the dead-end road that Nico felt inside.

"Don't you worry, Nickster," called one of the hockey players, Patrice? was that his name? Nico was wracking his brain, but his memory was fuzzy from the jolted sleep schedule and the last 48 hours. He'd been more social in the last two days than he had been in the last five years.

"We are going with you. You aren't facing that guy alone," he called. The other players nodded their agreement.

"The Gustopher fan club!" declared Nico, laughing.

"Not just that, man. It's all of you. We got you." 80%-certain-that's-Patrice said.

Nico's heart swelled at the welcoming wash of fraternity that came over him. He had hoped for such a feeling, clinging to it during his transition. It was such a simple gesture, and yet it meant the world to him. He spent several moments trying to collect himself. Jasper watched him, understanding and compassion filling his bright blue eyes. Jasper changed the subject to help him.

"I do think Brant confirmed last night with his detective friend that Mr. Rubra is still at the casino. I think we could leverage his love of the hockey team to at least see if he'll negotiate." Jasper looked at Nico sheepishly.

"Leverage, huh?" Nico said, raising an eyebrow at the question.

"Well, naturally, The Manley Cup and its affiliates can't be seen negotiating with a *known* criminal, but if our association will assist Gus, help him to see reason, then I — we want you to use it," Jasper said, reinforcing the sense of belonging that was growing in Nico.

"Thanks, that helps," Nico said, standing up. "I will go wake up Brant."

He called out to the kitchen, "Clean your plates!" as he climbed the stairs. Almost as an afterthought, he said, "Do it for Gus!"

"FOR GUS!" came the chorus below, as the sounds of clattering dishes followed Nico upstairs.

Saturday 7 pm

It had been several hours since the hockey players and Jasper had left Brant's with the Cup. They had elected to go back to their hotel room and wash up, promising to meet the guys at the casino later that night to show solidarity. Nico would call them when they hit the road.

Brant had woken late, closer to 3 pm, with Remi and Gus coming upstairs closer to dinnertime. Remi dashed out to grab a few birds for Gus— 'for the road' he had called out, gone in a flash — while Brant had filled in Nico on as many details that had been sorted, which was very little. Yes, he had confirmed that Viscidius would be at the casino. No, his detective friend couldn't help, as they had someone deep undercover right now, and couldn't risk a police presence. No, he hadn't come up with a brilliant plan. Yes, Nico had overheard several bizarre games and antics. Yes, they were probably all going to die.

Brant was just filling in Nico on Remi's cryptic comments when the chime in the grandfather's clock rang seven times. Remi was dashing back into the house as Brant said, "Well, this is it. We better get going."

As Nico made the brief call to Jasper and the hockey guys to let them know they were heading out, Remi was grinning like they were going for his favorite treat, his smile as broad as a cat studying an unsuspecting bird, just outside an open window.

CHAPTER 16

In an effort to make the beginning of the 90-minute drive more cheerful, the men now spoke comfortably about their lives. They were all noticeably more easy with each other, all trace of reservations had vanished. Nico was finally able to share a little bit about the process of transitioning, which both Brant and Remi were very supportive about. Remi was particularly astute, as he had known many trans people in his long life. Nico felt that when it came to male friendships, he had been mining away in a dark cavern, only to uncover multiple beautiful gems in the rough wall that fell into his hands easily. Nico also felt relaxed enough to chime in on the best practices for growing flora, both indoors and outdoors. He spoke a few times about the practice of bonsai, while Remi and Brant listened, enthralled.

Brant regaled them with the meditative practice of crochet and the benefit of the added finger dexterity. He expounded on his dreams of opening a bakery food cart and driving to the different food pods peppered throughout the city. He was rapturously describing making a gargoyle-shaped shortbread cookie while at the same time, musing out loud on how to manage both the fresh water and wastewater that is needed for sanitizing and baking. It was clear that being in the kitchen was where Brant felt his best.

Remi shared a story or two from his past about brief encounters with other gargoyles, — riveting tales, one of which involved running across London rooftops — but mostly listened attentively while occasionally reaching out to Gus in the back seat to touch his head, claws, and feet. They had bonded in their brief time on the roof and sleeping during the day, and it had softened his drive to sow mischief and chaos. Remi's eyes and face were relaxed, and his mouth wore a near-perpetual grin.

Each of them had such different personalities but seemed to enjoy being openly curious about each other's hobbies and lives.

And yet, to a man, they knew that their long evening was drawing to a close, and no one knew how to proceed after. In the silences between topics, the men exchanged glances of unspoken fears, each of them considering if they could find a drastic solution to avoid the confrontation. But even as a desperate idea would come to each of them, there wasn't time to iron out the logistics of making such a powerful enemy. Especially if they were trying to keep a baby gargoyle hidden at the same time. Besides, hiding wasn't in their nature.

As they drew closer to the casino, Nico and Brant grew quiet, while Remi had the gusto of a morning person who's just seen their umpteenth dawn and is still obnoxiously happy about it. He was whistling in the backseat, and Gustopher was babbling happily to himself. He also seemed to enjoy the night air and gazed out the partially open window, his eyes lost in daydream. It was Gus who now wore a serene, almost misty expression as they pulled into the expansive parking lot of the property, the giant "KRAKEN'S DEN" neon sign out front, perched over an arched walkway that led invitingly to the interior. *Den, oh, great,* thought Nico.

The casino and hotel were designed to allow easy and effortless entry, so the path leading in was wide, smooth, and opulent. It was the getting back out again that was the tricky bit.

Nico had a distinctly bad feeling about how a man such as Viscidius was going to take the news. Everything Nico had learned up until now was that he was wealthy, feared, opportunistic, and power-hungry. What he needed to know was if he was also ruthless. At the thought of Gus being taken, of being in the hands of someone who would treat him as a plaything in a menagerie, a cold certainty settled in Nico's stomach. He was not as quick on his feet as Brant. He wasn't deadly like Remi. He wasn't even as worldly as Jasper. But he loved that little guy, and despite the fact that he might be beaten unconscious or worse, he couldn't allow anything to happen to baby Gus.

Nico and Brant both gathered Gus, stashing him comfortably in the baby carrier on Brant. Nico surveyed the car seat and the various belongings strewn around the car. His heart thumped sadly looking at the back seats. How can such a little creature create such hominess in such a short time? In a fit of protection, he grabbed a pair of pruning shears from the trunk's gardening tools and stuffed them in his pocket.

Remi stood at the back of the car, as still as a granite pillar and clearly assessing the property. He turned back to the other two and spoke seriously.

"There is too much noise inside for me to hear anything, but there are four men posted at the front and several more inside. They smell of disgust and fear. They are expecting us, as they've been discussing us on their small radios," he reported, his lips curling in disapproval. Whether he disapproved of their security measures or their smell, Nico couldn't tell. It was probably both. There was no sign of the hockey players, and it was time. Nico said a silent prayer of thanks for their support from the night prior. He didn't blame them for not showing. It was terrifying, now that they were here.

As they approached the casino, the two men flanking the front made eye contact with Brant and nodded curtly. They also eyed Remi, but this was clearly wariness. Word of his supernatural talents had spread, likely after the attack on the car two nights prior. Remi had dropped all of his sly smiles, and his mischievous jokes, and was as serious as a blazing summer day in Phoenix. Nico knew that despite Remi's treatment of their journey as just an added entertainment to his own holiday, he genuinely cared for Gustopher and all of them. The guards didn't register Nico at all.

Remi flashed him an encouraging smile and winked so fast that Nico wasn't sure he had seen it. Remi's smile expanded, slowly revealing his fangs. The second two security guards they passed by on their walk inside saw this and took an instinctive step back. Nico felt braver and walked on with purpose through the doors. The four security guards closed rank, falling in behind them.

The casino was a symphony of bells, chimes, door alerts, low conversations, high conversations, clinks, and sighs. The greed hovered as a fine mist, lingering and coiling above every gambling table, and even thicker over the slot machines. The carpet was a calming blue with large hexagons, with a winding path of red hexagons cutting through it. It looked like the yellow brick road that Dorothy followed through Oz. Nico's brain briefly flitted to matching their personalities to those of the Tin Man, the Lion, and The Scarecrow, and repressed a laugh when he realized that Gus was Toto, the little dog.

Distracted, Nico saw a flash of something he recognized at the blackjack table and peered closer off to his left. It was a hockey jersey, and Nico recognized one of the players from the booth at the dance club where they had met Jasper. The player tipped his chin up in greeting at Nico, turning to another teammate to his right and saying something in confidence in his ear. He folded his hand at the table and walked off hastily before Nico had a chance to return the hello. Nico felt relief at seeing his friends, immediately followed by confusion. He was puzzled about why they had walked away when he spotted them.

As Nico returned his attention to their path, winding deeper and deeper into the casino, he saw that Brant had also recognized a few members of the hockey team off to the right, and something similar happened at the roulette table. Two hockey players recognized them and Gus, lifted their chin in acknowledgment, and quickly turned and walked away. Brant exchanged a confused glance with Nico, who shook his head. Remi led their group deeper, the lights growing darker as they approached a pair of matte-black double doors. The Kraken insignia was here again, carved out of wood into the door, but there was an oil stain-colored plaque above it that read "VIP Lounge."

There were another six guards here, and as they approached, the guards formed a front and back flank, trapping the four of them together. Among the six stood a tall, menacing-looking man who was clearly the head henchman.

Nico nearly laughed out loud. He was the picture of overzealous masculinity — his clothes, though casual, were tailored to the millimeter, and clung to his hewn frame. He wore a tight, dark grey turtleneck that hung to his mid-thigh with full-length sleeves, shiny black spandex leggings, and a weapons belt that looked like it held everything from kitchen scissors to a baton. He was attempting to give off every inch of do-not-mess-with-me, but his outfit was...confusing. He looked more like an angry ballet dancer/cat burglar than a security guard.

The man looked down, literally down into the baby carrier Brant had the kid in, and towered over Gustopher, who continued to look around in a bemused and sleepy manner, taking absolutely no notice of the inhospitable atmosphere developing. Brant's forearms and biceps were clenching almost in time at the man's close proximity and attempt to intimidate him, but he held his ground. Nico felt pride in his friend.

The other security goons took their cue from Angry Cat Burglar, but most of them already wore an expression of clear ridicule mixed with revulsion as the four of them approached the doors. One guard, however, whose arm was in a sling over her shoulder, held an expression of sadness and resignation. Nico noted her sympathetic smile at Gus.

"We are here to see Mr. Viscidius, to discuss this," Brant looked affectionately at Gus, "individual whom we found abandoned in the Emerald District. But if I could just ask first. Why the leggings?" The thugs around him shifted uncomfortably, a few of them even stifled laughs.

Angry Cat spat, "These are NOT leggings, you idiot! These are custom military-grade breeches from Russia and they can repeal heat sensors, are resistant to all forms of attack, such as biological, chemical, canine, amphibious, cyberwarfare —" he was interrupted by Brant.

"Cyberwarfare?" Brant asked, struggling to keep a straight face.

"Yes!" snapped Mr. Ballet Class Is Not Going Well. "Haven't you ever heard of nanobots?" he sneered at Brant as if this settled the debate.

"Yes, of course. But is that the kind of thing that's commonplace here in a casino?" Brant asked innocently. He was clearly toying with the man's patience.

"You can never be too careful." Mr. Not-Leggings said darkly, looking around the room as if nanobots were going to appear suddenly and attack him specifically. At least he was dressed for it. "The boss knows you are coming to return his —" he looked again at baby Gus, mistrust etched clearly on his face "— property." He looked as if he was about to say something further, but something was happening just behind Brant, and all the guards shifted their stances defensively.

Nico turned slightly to see behind the trio and was astonished to see over 15 hockey players all arrayed behind them in a row, each one wearing their jersey, with Jasper standing in the middle. The Manley Cup was next to him on a rolling table, and his hand rested protectively near the base. A crowd was forming behind them, buzzing with excitement, taking pictures, and drawing more attention.

"We thought you might need an escort," Jasper said, looking at Nico. His voice carried across the whole array and bolstered his friends. They exchanged quick, relieved glances. Jasper nodded firmly.

"Especially since these thugs don't know the first thing about Gus," a hockey player said, taunting the guards. Murmurs began to ripple among both sides; the goons were casting angry glances and beginning to shift about, their hands on weapons at their waists, ready to go on the offensive, and the hockey players began jeering and goading the guards further.

Jasper raised a hand. The players quieted. "It's your call," he said, his quiet voice carrying across the stand-off.

"We appreciate the support of the National Hockey Club," Nico said and paused, letting the weight of that be felt. "But we are here to do what's best for Gus. And that's a conversation to be held in private." He paused slightly. Gus looked up at him, quite alert now. Nico almost felt as if Gus was trying to communicate something important with his stare, but one of the guards spoke.

"You named that revolting thing? Gross. Not that it matters where he's going." One of the other guards elbowed him in the ribs, and he immediately quieted. This was exactly what Nico feared, but he said nothing.

Mr. Tights touched his finger to his earpiece. He nodded curtly to his group.

"Boss will see you now. Just you three. Not your...friends." He gestured to the two security guards closest to the doors to open them, and the wooden carving split apart, a crack of blue light crossing the floor, beckoning them in.

Chapter 17

Saturday 9 pm

As the doors opened, Nico could make out a large oval room. It was done in the same oil-stain colors as the door, with purple and blue and tinges of copper in the tabletops, chairs, artwork, and lighting. The overall effect was metallic and showy but with no warmth. There were two large, blue velvet booths, meant to seat large parties, not dissimilar to the booths at The Golden Knight. The room also contained a pool table and a petite bar tucked discretely to the right side of the room. There was a small DJ booth and a dance floor in the middle. The three of them made their way to the center of the dance floor, which felt like walking far too close to danger, but still a respectable distance from the booth where the owner sat. Nico wished that Jasper and the team could be with them, but felt their reassuring presence outside those double doors.

Viscidius Rubra sat at the back of one of the booths, his features just visible in the soft blue light cast around the room. He was an older white man in his mid-60s, with thinning hair and sallow skin. He wore a well-tailored but unremarkable black suit, a black shirt, and an electric blue tie. He had a sheaf of papers before him, a cigarette held in his slightly unsteady hand over an ashtray nearby. A crystal tumbler of what looked like bourbon was sweating slightly and gleamed in the darkness. The smell of cigarette smoke, old room service, and a lifetime of intimidating and bullying people permeated the space. Nico swallowed, trying to rinse his mouth of it; no luck. Viscidius was looking down at his papers as all the guards entered, both his security detail and the trio, with Gus hanging quietly in the baby carrier. Brant's hands were bouncing the baby's legs soothingly.

Remi sighed audibly behind them, clearly bored with the well-known tactic of trying to intimidate by feigning inattention. Nico had learned a great deal about men's body language by now, and he knew that a bored Remi was a dangerous one.

"Mr. Rubra. It's nice to finally meet you. My name is Nico. We have been looking for you, as I'm sure you know by now. There's been a terrible misunderstanding, so I'm grateful that you have the time to see us and clear it up." Nico was uncertain if Viscidius had even heard him, as he made no acknowledgment of their presence. He flicked a finger off to his right, and several of the black-clad guards came to stand at each side of his table, forming a protective wall. The rudeness and silence lengthened.

Finally, Viscidius Rubra spoke.

"How kind of you to defect from The Volcano to bring me my prize. When your former employer attacked my men three days ago — a misunderstanding, I assure you — this thing was left as a cost of doing business in someone else's territory. My men made a mistake by not going back," he snarled at the error, "I do want this animal for my menagerie. I had no idea you would take such dedication to return it to me. This creature has cost me a royal sum, so the loss was very, very disappointing.

"I don't suppose you are looking for a job? I could use such loyalty among my own associates." Viscidius pointedly let his gaze drift to the woman with the injured arm, who looked down in embarrassment.

Nico didn't like how this conversation was going. Viscidius thought of the three of them as people to be bought and traded, just like Gus. He clearly saw the little one as an exotic commodity, with value to be casually assessed and disregarded. He had no interest in Gus's well-being or safety. Nico wasn't surprised, and he knew he had to broach the subject at hand, but he didn't know how to say it without provoking him. A flash fire of rage erupted in his heart, but he kept his demeanor as cool as possible. He would not allow Gustopher to go to this man. He didn't care about the law, about the rights he may have, he only cared for Gus being with the people who loved him, the people that *he chose for himself* — his chosen family.

Add insult to injury, this man thought that he could tempt them to work for him? Nico had suspected that Viscidius treated all conversations opportunistically, but this was really taking the cake. Dios Mio, he was starting to think like Brant.

While Nico was processing his emotions, Brant, of course, had already sorted out his stance and stepped forward. *It was probably just as well,* thought Nico.

"Mr. Viscidius. My name is Brant. While I can say that we didn't expect such a generous offer, and it would be a privilege to work beside such fine associates of yours —" he glanced over his shoulder at Mr. Tight Pants and smiled broadly, "we must decline your offer."

Mr. Rubra tapped his cigarette irritably. He shook his head slowly as if in denial of Brant's words. Nico and Remi nodded their agreement. Nico was having trouble finding the words, but he knew that Remi was quiet out of a desire to not antagonize their host.

But Brant wasn't done.

"As far as turning over Gustopher to you," at this, Brant's face wore an easy, put-upon smile and Viscidius's eyes shifted to stare directly at him, "that's out of the question. We asked Gus, and he has decided he doesn't want to live his life in a cage. Or with you." He said this as respectfully as he could, but given that there was a clear tone of gleeful mocking underneath it, Nico gauged that it had landed like a brick in a mud puddle.

"That is *very* disappointing to hear, young man. Very disappointing, indeed. I don't think you grasp who you are talking to. I own that creature and have the papers to prove it. All you are doing is delaying the inevitable, and making an enemy of me in the process. That thing is the star of my menagerie and will take its rightful place so I can show it off to my clients. Your reach extends your grasp." He said this in a tone that clearly ended the conversation, while again gesturing with his hand to his men to take the gargoyle.

It was at this point that Gus woke up. As in, fully woke up. His eyes were wider than Nico had ever seen them. A glow had appeared along his spine, shining through his gray reptilian skin. Ripples of flashing colors were cascading down his legs and arms. His ear tips were a pearlescent white. He was fidgeting in the carrier, desperate to be let down. Brant could barely contain him, and Gus reached up to hoist himself over the contraption that held him to Brant. He landed on all fours, facing Rubra and the men clustered around him. They began to draw their weapons, but Viscidius shook his head, still wanting to retrieve Gustopher alive.

Nico, Brant, and Remi were uncertain what was happening, but if Gus felt he was in danger, they would protect him. Remi turned his back, guarding their flank. Brant ripped the carrier from his body and threw it aside, planted his stance, and balled his fists. Nico dug frantically in his pockets for the shears, anything that could help protect him. He brandished them before him like a knife, keenly aware that while he didn't know how to use them for anything other than trimming leaves, it was still a blade, and Rubra's men didn't know what he could do. Or in this case, not do.

But Gus didn't need help. He paced back and forth, the colors swirling angrily on his small body. His ears were smoking now, the white light curling up like a thread of church incense, disappearing into the ceiling. Nico saw a ripple of colors shudder up his small back and lead towards his mouth, where he opened his jaws and let out a huge curl of blue-hot fire.

The fire caused the men surrounding their boss to dive and scatter to the sides of the room. Viscidius dove under the table, cowering on the booth's filthy and cocktail napkin-strewn floor. The men behind them facing Remi clustered near the doorframe, huddled out of fear. Even without Remi's supernatural smell, Brant could smell the sour urine on several of the men, the dank smell permeating the space quickly. *Viscidius must have had the fire sprinklers disabled in this room so he could smoke,* thought Brant. That was a mistake, clearly. The woman with the injured arm and the bartender together both ran hastily for a hidden service door and glancing at the trio, ran through it and abandoned the security detail. Gus was circling the trio, keeping a good three foot wall of fire between them and Viscidius's men. But Brant did note that Gus was careful not to set anything on fire. He was just forming a protective barrier. *He's too smart, he's going to be such a handful,* Brant considered.

Gus was roaring at the same time as delivering his fireball, and while Remi was certain it wouldn't be heard outside the room in terms of volume, it was a reverberating sound like a 70 hz bass frequency underneath it. It vibrated Remi's fangs in a way he did *not* enjoy, but at the same time, was getting enormous pleasure out of watching a 30 lb. lizard protect his foster dads when they had been ludicrously swaddling him for three nights. Gustopher was a magnificent beast and had no need of it. It had been a joy to watch him twist these men around his smallest claw.

Remi knew that gargoyles were clever, had unique communication skills, and could transform, but the fire thing in one so young was new to him. He stepped cautiously up behind Gus while he was circling, alerting the angry creature with his body language that they were safe, and while the state of the bad guys was indeed very amusing, Gus could probably put the fire out now. He nudged Gus with his foot, very gently. Gus stopped his unearthly bassy roar with added barbeque feature and turned to look up at Remi, his tongue hanging happily out the side. His eyes were triumphant. Remi smiled at him and began to laugh.

Chapter 18

Saturday 9:15 pm

Viscidius indicated feebly from under the table to let the four of them go, with an insistence that bordered on hysteria that the trio leave the casino and take Gus with them. Now. Please.

Nico was shaken by the events in the VIP Lounge, following the red hexagonal carpet in a daze while holding a pair of pruning shears by his side. Nico looked at Brant with his eyebrows raised over what just happened, but Brant just shook his head back at him, clearly saying "Not now." The hockey players were all still waiting outside the double doors, but several of them had clapped their hands over their ears and were looking very dazed.

Jasper was beaming at Gus, who toddled over to him and allowed himself to be scooped up by the trophy guard. Jasper set Gus down in the top of the Manley Cup — the highest possible honor, usually only reserved for team captains — and Gus looked so smug, that the players began cheering and punching their fists in the air like they had won the championship all over again. Nico and Brant were visibly relieved to still see them there. Remi was the only composed one. Brant and Nico had linked arms over each others' shoulders, shaking their heads in disbelief and making incoherent noises of astonishment.

A few moments later, the woman with the injured arm approached them cautiously and caught Nico's eye. Nico hugged Brant and stepped to the side to talk to her.

"Hey. I'm Paula. I just wanted to say that I'm glad the little dude is doing okay. Seems to be doing more than okay, from what I saw." She smiled affectionately at Gus, still looking superior atop the giant silver cup. Gus was allowing the players to touch him, his eyes back to a contented gaze. The colors still rippled subtly across his back. Nico needed to find out what *that* was about.

"No thanks to your side," Nico said evenly. "Still, yes, he seems to be able to hold his own, which is a great relief." Nico conceded.

"Yeah, I was never okay with my boss trying to keep him. That's why I put my son's car seat in the back, instead of putting that kid in a cage," she said, one hand running through her short hair nervously. "Didn't seem right, keeping him locked up."

Nico replied, encouraging, "You did the right thing. But why are you working for this guy? He's bad news," Nico said.

"Oh, that's over now. I quit," Paula laughed. "Between my sprained arm and this, I can't work here." she gestured to the scene in front of him, her eyes crinkling into a smile.

"Well, best of luck to you. Thanks for not fighting us, I guess." Nico wasn't sure what the right thing to say was.

"Well, it was a no-brainer, really. Sometimes in security, you guard valuable things, but your values have to be guarded as well." Paula said, then began musing aloud. "There's a big difference between being a guard and being security. Security comes from a fear born of past hurts. It involves shielding and masking. It's reactive. But true guarding is wisdom in knowing heartbreak will happen again, and being prepared to respond from a place of love. It involves tools. It's proactive," she said and walked away.

Nico was struck by the casual philosophy. Sometimes people could really communicate deep things with such brevity. He took a note of the woman's nametag and headed back over to all his new friends.

Saturday 10 pm

On their way out of the casino, the hockey team accompanied them in case Viscidius changed his mind and sent his goons after them, but there was no disturbance. They walked the trio back to their car, and everyone gave Gus an affectionate pat on the head or shoulders, some of them even fist/claw-bumping him in solidarity. Gustopher was clearly in his happy place, as the colors continued to shimmer lightly across his back.

Brant and Nico stared at Remi. Finally Brant said, "Exactly — and pardon my French here — what the hell was that?"

"What do you think, mon petit chou?"

"I think that our little Gus behaved exactly like a —"

"Yes. Go on!"

"— I mean, that was more like a —" Brant reasoned, glancing at Nico, who was nodding.

"— You are so close, mon bebe Brie!"

"— a dragon? Are you saying Gustopher is a DRAGON?" Brant said, astonished.

And Remi replied with complete sincerity, "Oui, a dragon."

Brant and Nico turned to each other and burst out laughing. The kind of hysterical laughter that comes with denial, begrudging acceptance, a cleansing cry, and then collapsing for a long nap. But neither of them could nap yet. They needed to get clear of the casino first. It had been a long, long, eventful evening, and getting Gus to sleep was the next plan of action.

Jasper had spent a good 15 minutes holding Gus at the car and was clearly reluctant to let him go. Nico could see the struggle in his face as his duty to the Cup was warring with his paternal instincts. He finally handed Gus back over to Remi, but Remi shook his head, saying, "My vacation is at an end, and it's time for me to go home. I have absolutely adored getting to know the little one, and I'm certain there are more surprises in store, but for now, he chooses the two of you."

"More surprises? Remi, please." Brant said, clutching his chest. "My heart can't take it."

Nico looked at Remi thoughtfully. "Will we be able to reach you somehow?"

Remi studied the bonsai bodyguard, his face relaxing into one of his impish grins.

"You know that dragons keep hordes, right?"

"I guess. I mean, that's a popular myth. I'm not sure what's real or myth anymore, to tell you the truth. The last three days have taught me that myths might not be so fictional after all," Nico said, gazing at Gustopher who was now in Brant's arms. The baby was waving his claws around in circles.

"And what do you think sweet Gus is gathering for his horde?" Remi prompted Nico. He was back in professor mode.

Nico faltered, "I'm not sure." He decided to roll the dice and try the direct approach. "What do you think he's collecting, Remi?"

Remi's smile broadened, revealing his fangs. If Nico didn't know him, he would say it was menacing, but as it were, it was just sweet, corny Remi. "Oh, my dear sweet Sancerre, your adventure has just begun. Gustopher collects good men, of course. And yes, I'll be in touch."

Remi reached out and stroked the dragon's head, pulling on of the ears gently.

"Just you wait until you find out about Gustopher's *other* magic abilities," he said winking, and took off running. He didn't say goodbye to anyone else, just *poof*, he was gone.

Brant and Nico stood in the kind of disbelieving shock of people who found out not only did they win the lottery, but that they had won two lotteries.

Because it wasn't until this moment that they had really considered what came next. Gus wasn't in danger. And they had all survived.

Nico looked at Brant.

Brant looked back at his friend.

They both looked at Gustopher.

The dragon grinned like a goofy monster at them both, his eyes shining with love and mischief. He had the bright, manic-eyed look of an exhausted toddler who still had plans to keep his parents up for another 24 hours.

Brant finally sighed and spoke.

"Do you think Babies R Us is open yet?"

Epilogue

It was a beautiful Spring day in Multnomah six months later when Nico stepped out his front door, waving a hand at an impatiently-honking Brant from his blue battered truck parked across the street. Only recently Nico had started holding Gus's claw as Gus navigated stairs, but the kid pulled away in order to clumsily handle them on his own, attempting to walk them on two legs and then giving up and going to four legs in frustration. Gus always wanted to be near one, or preferably both, of his dads.

Brant popped out of the truck and leaned down to eye level with Gus and gestured for him to walk to him, but Gus was enjoying a four-legged canter across the slick street, so he ran head first into Brant and knocked him over. Brant gave out a deep chuckle of happiness and squeezed the baby tightly.

Just then, a two-door sedan pulled up behind Brant's truck, crawling to a walking speed near the duo, maneuvering cautiously next to the street curb. A woman they both recognized approached the three, a smile hovering at the corners of her mouth.

"Am I late?" she said nervously.

"Not at all. We are just heading out." Brant said easily. He transferred Gus over to the woman who took him with the seasoned firmness of someone who's been around kids before.

"When I reached out to you guys after what happened at the casino, I didn't think you'd take my call," she said in a low tone, looking at both men.

Nico sighed, exasperated. "Paula, we've been over this. You were kind to Gus from the get-go. You met him properly last week. It's just a few hours of babysitting. That job really messed with you. Don't worry, it's cool. We like you. He likes you. Go to therapy." Nico said this last bit with a smile, but Paula knew he also meant it.

Brant turned to Nico. "Are you ready? Got all the paperwork?" he asked, anxiously. It wasn't like Brant to worry, and it amused Nico to have switched roles, even temporarily. He was the confident, calm one today. And of all days, today it was especially important to have a cool game face on. It was a big day for all of them, and hopefully, nothing was going to go wrong.

Nico nodded and gestured at the business portfolio in his hands. It contained all the paperwork they had obtained from Rubra to transfer the "exotic pet permit" of Gustopher over to Nico and Brant for joint custody. They had spent the winter outfitting their house — Nico had moved in almost immediately to Brant's — obtaining a steady food source, and keeping Gus comfortable while they sorted through the legalities. Viscidius had filed the permit that Gus was an "exotic lizard" because, at the time, Gus was extremely lethargic and of no interest to the state's Department of Fish and Wildlife administrative staff. Viscidius had bribed his way through the permit process because following the law was not his style.

If the Department had gotten word of a new species, namely a dragon who could breathe fire, all hell would break loose. Nico and Brant wanted to secure themselves as his legal guardian before the scientific community tried to classify him, run tests on him, and in general, keep him separated. Not to mention what might happen if the military found out.

They waved goodbye to Gus and Paula, and headed towards the drab government building that would change their fate. *What was that phrase?* thought Nico. *'When God pays attention to you, it's with a kiss and a slap.'* He felt like he'd already been slapped. Maybe this was the kiss part?

Nico rolled the windows down. It was too nice of a day out not to.

"Do you think they'll ask about breeding? As far as we know, he's the only one of his kind, right?" Nico asked. Now Brant's nerves were leaking over to him. Shit.

Brant piped up. "I've memorized the main concerns." He began to recite the permit code. This had been Brant's obsession for the past few weeks, memorizing any and all state codes that could threaten their chances at not keeping Gus. Brant was taking no chances that something as mundane as a government employee or laws would come between him and his kid.

"Except as provided in subsection (4) of this section, 609.341, a person keeping an exotic animal in this state may not breed that animal." He rattled off without thinking. Nico was impressed with his recall ability, but since it had ramped up the stress level of the whole situation, he didn't show it.

"So, no little baby Gus, I guess? Frankly, I think we have our hands full with this one." Nico remarked wryly.

Twenty minutes later, they had pulled into the building's parking garage and were on their way up to the 3rd floor. There was a deeply depressing elevator covered top to bottom in 1970s fake wood paneling. They exited the elevator and followed signs to the permitting office, where they sat in the lobby after taking a number from a kiosk. Brant's legs were going a mile a minute, bobbing up and down with the nervous staccato of an engine piston. "Ginger. Cardamom. Black pepper and chili flakes," he muttered under his breath. Nico had long since learned that Brant was comforted by reciting ingredients of his favorite baked goods to himself when he was out of sorts.

"Number 18," Nico heard a bored voice call out, and he rose out of his seat, pulling a distracted Brant with him. "What? Oh! Is it time?" Brant said lowly. He smoothed his button-down shirt, his muscles straining the sleeves. Brant was also not used to wearing business clothes.

"Application paperwork and I.D., please," said the employee, not once breaking eye contact from their computer screen.

"We are applying for an exotic pet permit transfer. Here's all the paperwork. My I.D. is on top there." Nico replied, passing the portfolio to them under the bulletproof glass.

"Oh. Is that all? You didn't need to come down here. You could've done that online. Would've taken you 10 minutes, tops. What is it, a puma or somethin?" they said, looking down and pulling out their transfer of ownership application. They barely glanced at the paperwork, only pointing to three spots on the application where Nico and Brant had both carefully initialed in the correct places. Nico didn't trust himself to answer, as they had agreed not to give out any information that wasn't strictly necessary to the permitting process.

"Ah. Joint ownership. Okay. One sec, you two." They walked away with the application, and Brant shoved Nico in the arm, hard. Nico winced, and Brant mouthed a "sorry" as the employee walked to a back table, took out a giant stamp, and made an ominous ka-chunk noise, before returning to the window a few minutes later. Nico and Brant both sucked in their breath instinctively, but their paperwork had a bright green ACCEPTED stamped across it, obscuring their names. Nico's heart swelled, warmth and adrenaline coursing through his body. He gripped the counter ledge so hard his fingertips started to turn white.

Brant shoved him again in the shoulder, but it was a scantily contained, joyful kind of shove. The employee finished tapping on their keyboard and passed the portfolio back to Nico because Brant had moved away to do the most reserved foot scuffle Nico had ever seen. The employee also passed over some more permit renewal paperwork that doubtlessly Brant had already memorized and recited to him in the last few months.

Nico thanked the employee, and they both calmly walked down the stairs, through the main lobby, and out to the parking garage. They stood outside the truck, jumping up and down with wild abandon, shouting with relief, and hugging out their joy and triumph of finally making Gus their own.

Acknowledgements

None of this book would be possible without the support and love of my own chosen family and friends.

Special and outstanding recognition is due to everyone who donated to my fundraiser.

<u>Those exemplary humans are</u>

Stephanie Keller, Dan Fedorenko, Niccole Paytosh, Dan Franco, Ra Vermel, the Zimmerman family, Brandon Newton, Tess Snook O'Riva, Julia Wilson, Rae Crothers, Sarah McCaleb, Kathryn DiFoxfire Wilson, Wendy Caesar, Danetta Jackson, Jazzmyne Gregoire, Anne Gearhart, Elizabeth Veervort, Michelle Meeker, Team Woodbury, Celeste Larson, Lydia Aretis, Staci & Dan Herrick, Brenda Kahler, and Rose Puigmarti.

The team who helped me bring the story from scribbles to elegant script is so talented in each of their own ways.

<u>Those extraordinary humans are:</u>

Mentoring up close, Rebecca Thorne. Mentoring from afar, Travis Baldree. Alpha readers, Cat Johnston and Anne Gearhart. Beta readers, Stephanie Bjelland, Amy Cocke, Cyn, K.C. Sensitivity readers, RoAnna Sylver and Rina Amaranthine (@liquidrina). Editor, Phoebe M. Liu (AKA Crab) of Crab Editing. Cover artist, Indiana Maria Acosta Hernandez, alias Indicreates. Typographer, Amphi Studio. Formatter, J. Houser. Marketing, Haley Pollock, Legit PA Services. Web design, Caleb Poole.

This book was written via Campfire Writing. I employed techniques from NaNoWriMo. I used the Stanford Breath font for cover and interior titles. To protect my intellectual property, I used Muso.com. I leaned heavily on the teachings of both Travis Baldree and his article on Medium.com, as well as empowered mentoring from

Rebecca Thorne. I used Portland, Oregon as inspiration for the region and city.

The treasure hunt map was built using Google Maps. I made the gargoyle icons myself using Canva Pro.

And lastly, I want to especially thank my partners Brennan and Chris Brecheen, to whom I called many, many, many times to gush about the process, some new inspiration, to wave at them, essentially, from the roller coaster car while I plummeted through a pool of water, giggling the entire time.

Names & Pronunciations

The city of Multnomah is so named because it is the origin name that multiple Native tribes used for thousands of years of this area along the now-named Willamette River. The name of the river has also been restored in the book to the Whilamut River, from the Kalapuyan word "Whilamut" which means "Where the river ripples and runs fast."

You can read more about the history of Native tribes in this area of the Pacific Northwest here —https://www.oregonhistoryproject.org/

People

Gustopher — (Gus-tuh-fer)

Nico — (Nee-koh)

Brant — (Brant)

Remi — (Re-mee)

Jasper — (Jas-per)

Viscidius Rubra — (Vis-sid-ee-us Roo-bra)

Patrice — (P-uh-t-r-EE-s)

Xavi — (Zha-vee)

Paula — (Paw-luh)

Locations

City of Multnomah — (Mult-nom-mah)

Whilamut River — (Wheel-a-moot)

MinnWild — (Min-wild)

The Golden Knight — (Gold-en Nyt)

The Kraken's Den — (Kr-a-ken)

Other

Camorra — (kuh-mor-uh)

Riders of Ohan — (Oh-han)

Nanny Ogg — (Nan-nee Og)

Bonsai Tips

The cut-and-develop method was the original basic technique of training bonsai before wiring was used. This training method depends heavily on pruning to style and train the tree. Although that seems simple enough, you do need to understand pruning and ramifications to use this technique successfully.

Our top 3 bonsais for this technique are Elms, Fukien Tea trees, and Hornbeams.

Some of the tools you will need include: pruning shears, concave branch cutters, root rake, and cut paste.

There are a few bonsai schools and even bonsai enthusiasts to this day who prefer only to use clip-and-grow bonsai techniques as it's a more natural approach to training and styling your tree.

Very basically put, the cut-and-develop technique is exactly as the name suggests. You let the branches grow out long and then cut back to the desired length, usually just before two buds and where wood has already formed in the branch or stem.

New growth will then sprout from the buds in a new direction. Once again, leave the new growth to grow out nice and long, giving enough time for the wood to form in the stems before cutting back again.

Summary:
    Let the branches grow
    Inspect branches for signs of wood growth
    Clip back the branches

Prune away branches where 3 or more shoots develop from the same buds

Using the bonsai clip-and-grow technique allows the tree to guide you in the style and design and let nature take its course. In the end, you'll have a beautifully natural-styled bonsai with great taper, texture, and thick trunk.

Original article by Leri Koen — https://tinyurl.com/2x73p9aj

RECIPE

Parmesan-Herb Madeleines

Prep Time 10 minutes || Cook Time 10 minutes
Total Time 20 minutes
Servings 24 mini madeleines

Ingredients

- 1/3 cup UNBLEACHED ALL-PURPOSE FLOUR
- 1 teaspoon BAKING POWDER
- 1/4 teaspoon SEA SALT
- 1 LARGE EGG lightly beaten
- 1/3 cup NONFAT PLAIN YOGURT
- 1/4 cup 1 OUNCE FRESHLY GRATED PARMIGIANO-REGGIANO (OR GRUYERE)
- 1 tablespoon FINELY MINCED FRESH ROSEMARY or chives

Instructions

Preheat your oven to 425°F. I recommend spraying your madeleine pan with nonstick spray even if it's already labeled as nonstick.

Using a food processor, combine the ingredients from the flour to the yogurt and blend well. Add the cheese and rosemary and process until combined.

Spoon the batter onto the madeleine molds and bake in the center rack of your oven for about 10 minutes or until firm and golden. Cool the madeleines for a few minutes before serving. Serve warm or at room temperature (I prefer them warm).

The following recipe was borrowed by Brant who first saw it on the Lemon and Anchovies online blog, who reposted it from Patricia Wells' *The Provence Cookbook,* **Savoury Rosemary-Parmesan Madeleines**

Original recipe — https://tinyurl.com/2hd84jrs

Cheese Caves 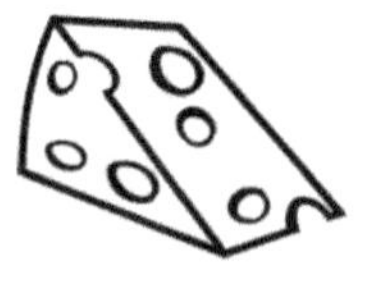

In 1949, the USDA introduced the Dairy Product Price Support Program, later known as the Milk Price Support Program. When the price of dairy products sunk too low for farmers, the USDA would offer to buy up the excess at a stable rate. It bought millions of pounds of cheese, butter, and dry milk from producers who would otherwise have lost a lot of money if they only relied on their regular retailers. The result? The dairy market would stabilize, producers would have steady income and prices for the products would eventually rise. Then, once the prices of dairy products hit 125 percent of the support price, the USDA would start selling off its stash in bulk.

That wasn't so great either. The USDA buying up cheese prevented the prices from dipping too low—but the department also put a ceiling on how high the prices could climb. "This is especially true during the 1980s. You ended up with prices not able to move out of either end of the spectrum," explains Scott Brown, an agricultural economist at the University of Missouri. "It did create very stable prices. But most folks weren't very happy with that kind of operation, and it was costly [for the government]."

Now, the USDA had to pivot. It started reducing the support prices and buying less stock, but that didn't have a huge impact. So it moved to the next phase: getting rid of the automatic sell triggers. Instead of selling out its stores of dairy products when market prices climbed to 125 percent of the support price, it would leave it up to the secretary of agriculture to decide when to release the product. "That became a political football, how to handle the release of stocks," Brown says. Not only that, but if the secretary of agriculture decided to hold on to stores past the previous 125-percent cutoff, stocks would keep accumulating. The cheese and butter and dry milk would pile up, and then the USDA would have to scramble to deal with them before they spoiled.

It was a tricky balance to strike. Eventually, the USDA decided it had had enough, ending the price support program in 2014. But it kept hoarding cheese and still does so to this day. Only now, it's for use in food assistance programs. In the latest cold storage report, the USDA shows a little less than 1.5 billion pounds of cheese in storage, along with 355 million pounds of butter, 211 million pounds of pecans and just less than a billion pounds of french fries (it stores a lot of stuff!).

Original article by Emily Baron Cardloff —
https://tinyurl.com/ymwh2szj

Stanley Cup History

Why is it called the Stanley Cup?

The Stanley Cup is named after Lord Stanley of Preston, (in this book, Lord Manley) the Governor General of Canada in 1892.

He purchased a decorative cup that was eventually donated in order for it to be awarded to the top amateur hockey team in Canada. Stanley and his family had fallen in love with the sport of hockey after viewing games at the 1889 Winter Carnival in Montreal.

The Cup bounced around a number of leagues before the NHL took a firm hold of professional hockey in North America. By 1926, the Cup was only given out to NHL teams and in 1947, the NHL reached an agreement with Cup trustee J. Cooper Smeaton to grant total control of the Stanley Cup to the NHL.

How old is the Stanley Cup?

The Stanley Cup was first awarded in the 1892–93 season.

It is the oldest trophy that can be won by professional athletes in North America.

How heavy is the Stanley Cup?

The Stanley Cup weighs 34.5 pounds or 15.5 kilograms.

It is 35.25 inches tall, which is 89.64 centimeters.

How many Stanley Cups are there?

There are technically three Stanley Cups.

The first one, the original one purchased by Lord Stanley, was awarded until 1970. Clarence Campbell, who was the president of the NHL at the time, felt as though the original was becoming too brittle to be passed around to championship teams. Now that Cup, which is referred to as the Dominion Hockey Challenge Cup, is on display in the Hockey Hall of Fame.

The current cup, called the Presentation Cup, is the trophy that is given out to the championship teams. There is a Hockey Hall of Fame seal at the bottom that confirms its authenticity.

The final cup is a replica of the Presentation Cup. It was created in 1993 to be used as a stand-in at the Hall of Fame when the Presentation Cup is not available.

Original article by Bryan Murphy of Sporting News —
https://tinyurl.com/2fbwdvkh

Book 2 Sneak Peek

An exclusive look into Book 2 of The Gus Chronicles, "What to Suspect when You're Suspecting"

The smoke was rising in the morning air from the pit. Huge, white puffy clouds ringed with green and silver, stark against the blue sky. Gus watched from a distance as the humans gathered the dead into wheelbarrows, scraps of fabric tied around their pitiful mouths against the stench and carried the bodies ungently, dropping them into the pit on the outskirts of the village. A putrid, evil human would drop a torch into the pit and Gus would watch the fire rise slowly. Again.

Xe (footnote 1) watched this display with a vast and empty heart. The grief was too large, it swallowed xer whole and left only a frail spine to hold together it's claws and ears, it's tail and legs. How could xe keep trying? It had been so long in the reckoning of human time, something that dragons didn't bother to measure. What a human called a day, a dragon called a year, so what was this, to xer?

It was not the first time, but someday, it would be the last. Xe swore this again, as if the last swearing — and the one before that, and the one before that — hadn't been in vain. There was a time, in a different country when the ice had covered more of the land, when the presence of good men — something that manifested across all types of humans, wasn't so shunned. Wasn't so hated and feared. Humans were so stupid at times. They had such quick brains, so quick, that their thoughts leapt like a monkey at a branch, miscalculating and falling down. And instead of choosing a branch closer or stronger, they chose the brittle, thin branch. One that you could barely stand on, and for what? Even as you stood,

Footnote 1: Dragons identify themselves as gender fluid. Their pronouns are as follows: Xe ("pr. Zee") Xer ("pr. Zer") Xers ("pr. Zers") Xerself ("pr. Zer-self") *high on that brittle branch of thought, no leaves or other creatures to play and enjoy life with you, they looked down from their branch on high, spitting and shivering from the cold. Alone.*

But most of the monkeys enjoyed the shelter of stronger branches, those with boughs, and built cozy nests. They had each other, they were warm, and they were closer to the ground to forage for food.

Gus loved that time with humans. Dragons were smaller then, closer in size as to xer size now. They hunted with humans, played games with them, splashed in the water and explored the mountains, caves, and deserts. Along with the wolves, dragons were the best of friends to the humans. For everyone on those lower branches. life was delightful, simple, and full of joy. Gus missed those times and was determined to bring back some semblance with xer magics. Gus would never stop trying to gather good men despite the outcome.

But some monkeys just had to stand above the others.

When the humans got a hold of the idea of shame, it was only a matter of time before they came for the ones they perceived as different. The women-men. The men-women. The multi-gender. The no-sex. Gus didn't know what they called it; Gus didn't care. Dragons didn't see gender and sex this way. Whatever was seen in nature was natural. No other species questioned this. Humans decided they had a WAY that was special, something that could set them apart.

What was so great about 'apart'? Gus wondered, for the millionth time. Apart is what led to this. Pointless, tragic, cruel death of xer beloved ones, now ashes in a pit. Gus had loved those humans. Gus had raised and considered those humans family. But these humans, the ones who were left? They were not kin.

All thoughts of vengeance had drained from xer mind. It was not worth fighting with these petty humans about. They would not see reason. They didn't even welcome the telepathic communication that the wolves

Xe would transform again, reduce size (despite how painful and the enormous magic it took) and hibernate. Xe would wait a few hundred years and come back, drawing those good men close to xer. Xe would try again to show the humans — the stupid ones —that good men could change their world. Gus had seen it.

Gus awoke from another terrible memory-dream with the acrid smell of death and smoke, and xe *hated* it. Xe climbed the stairs, magic weak in xer limbs, and lumbered over to xer human, the plant one, climbing into his lap and getting a little snuggle.

"Well, hi there. Rough night again?" Nico said softly. He had been journaling and set aside the pen and notebook on a nearby wooden side table. The soft colors from the spring sunset were permeating the broad front window, and Gus's eyes closed briefly in clear weariness.

"Do you want some breakfast, or do you want to play first?" Nico's eyes drifted encouragingly to a mat set up on the floor in the kitchen. The mat was an irregular shaped grid made up of hexagonal bases. On top of the hexagons was a big round electric button on each. They were set up in groups by color, so the red, blue, green, and yellow sections all represented different subjects. Nico pointed to the mat, trying to get Gus to use the buttons to communicate. Brant and Nico had both learned that despite the fact that Gus could sometimes use his mouth to speak, it drained his energy. Gus was never going to speak full sentences. Since they were in new territory on how to communicate, Brant had seen these at the pet store while buying some birds and decided to give it a try.

Gus glanced at the mat, which he normally enjoyed, but didn't move. Nico pointed a hand, encouraging Gus again. "Will you at least tell me if you are hungry? It's good practice." Nico smiled gently at Gus. Gus sighed and clambered out of Nico's lap. Xe hunted for the correct button to tell plant man what xe wanted. Xe located the yellow button and pressed it four times, deliberately pausing each time to punctuate xer intent.

Nico laughed from the living room. "Okay, okay, I get it. 'Hug, hug'. I hear you." Nico stood from the soft armchair and came over, scooping up Gus in his arms.

"Oofta. You are getting big." Nico said, straining a little to shift Gus to his hips.

Knock, knock, knock! a sound came from the front door, the one they never used, as using the back door was always easier to access the car from the side driveway.

Knock, knock, knock! came again, this time more aggressively.

Brant appeared suddenly, entering the room quietly and stealthy, gesturing for Nico and Gus to move away from the window. Brant's face was set in hyperawareness. Nico heard a stern male voice call from the front door.

"This is General Malcolm Hatworth from the U.S. Army. We want to speak with you about your...ward."

Discussion Questions

There are several themes in Guarding Gus that will be explored throughout the trilogy. These questions are meant to function as a guide for discussion among friends, family, and book clubs. Caution! There are spoilers ahead.

1. The question of Gustopher's rights is a major and immediate question of the book. Gus is an animal but also sentient, is able to communicate, and a member of a magical species. What parallels can you draw to non-domesticated animals in our world? What is the danger in having some exotic animals as pets?

2. The presence of a trans man is accepted in this book, but there are some experiences Nico has that are typical for trans men that might've been new to you. For instance, the initial handshake with Brant. Did you notice that interaction? Why would it be difficult for Nico to shake Brant's hand?

3. Brant is a former soldier and is struggling to return to life as a civilian. Most of his adult life, his identity was centered around military rules both spoken and unspoken. In times of duress, Brant often relies on his skills and training to facilitate the scenario, whether it's friendly or hostile. Do you think this serves him or it will cause damage in the long run? What is Brant at risk of losing the more he relies on his military persona?

4. Gus is assigned a male identity by Nico and Brant early in the book. Did you agree with this decision or their logic? How would you have handled the question of addressing

a new entity whose culture and identity you know nothing about?

5. The themes of positive masculinity is a major component of the people surrounding Gus. When Gus is in the presence of more rigid masculinity, they are repelled by the gargoyle. Why is that? Why aren't women experiencing such strong reactions to Gus?

6. Another theme of the book is consent. Gus's persuasive magic <u>can</u> be resisted, but must be actively done so, otherwise it's like casting a spell on someone against their will. Gus also communicates with a nonverbal refusal of going to Rubra by flying out of the car. How did these instances of consent resonate with you?

Other Offerings

Other Offerings by Promise Press

Romance/Autobiographical fiction:
Stockings Required, Tales of a Cigarette & Candy Girl

The Spicy Coloring Book series:
Stabby Feelings: a Humorous Floral Swearing Coloring Book for Adult Stress Relief
Fucking Brilliant: An Empowerment Coloring Book
How Dare You: A Humorous, Scandalous Coloring Book

Halloween coloring books:
Perky Goth Halloween Coloring Book: Vol 1 & 2

Self-Help:
Intention Coloring: Color Your Goals into Reality

Go to www.promisepress.org for even more items!